In for a Penny: A partially paranormal romance

by

Shelley White

In for a Penny, Book 3

In for a Penny: a partially paranormal romance

COPYRIGHT © 2022 by Shelley E White

Cover Art by *The Wild Rose Press, Inc.*

The Wild Rose Press, Inc.
PO Box 708
Adams Basin, NY 14410-0708
Visit us at www.thewildrosepress.com

Publishing History
First Edition, 2023
Trade Paperback ISBN 978-1-5092-4641-0
Digital ISBN 978-1-5092-4642-7

In for a Penny, Book 3
Published in the United States of America

Dedication

To John, with all my love.
To Ally, with all my appreciation.
To the readers who've made it all the way to book
three, thank you and I hope you've enjoyed Penny's
story.

Chapter 1

Fang it!

"Here it is!" Bobbie said, presenting us with the third and hopefully final book in my family legacy fulfillment quest. The legacy that dumped me into the plot of whatever book I happened to read in order to meet my supposed true love.

Chase the Night was an indie-published paranormal romance, which Bobbie highly recommended. Since I wasn't currently able to do any recreational reading myself, I had to take her word for it. She was pretty picky about her reading material, so though this whimsical choice surprised me, I trusted her judgment.

We were sitting in the reading nook of my shop, *Penny Pincher Used Books*. Please don't assume I'd actually named the store after myself. My grandmother, the store's original owner, did me that dubious honor. So even though I cringe a little inside every time I hear the name, I can't bear to change it. I'm not clinging sadly to all my grandmother's old possessions, but I am keeping the shop name. Every time I hear it, I also think of Gram.

I'd given Tripp, the object of my affection, the book information and he'd ordered himself a copy from Amazon. It hadn't come in yet, but it didn't really matter; I'd be reading us both in for this first go.

I stared at the book in her hands with trepidation.

"The title's kind of corny, isn't it?"

"It's fairly genre standard. You can't take paranormal romance too seriously, after all." Bobbie jutted her chin out defensively.

"No, no. That's fine. I trust your judgment."

Bobbie pursed her lips.

"All right! Let's do this thing!" Peter, Bobbie's boyfriend said with surprising enthusiasm.

"Hold up a minute. Let me go over it one more time. I know I'm the novice vampire hunter, and Tripp's the vampire. Who will everyone else be?" I asked. Tripp was actually super-excited about his role. He looked forward to having super strength and speed; the fangs, not so much. We weren't yet sure if any of the supernatural stuff would actually work, so I hoped Tripp wouldn't be too disappointed if he was just a regular human-strength vampire.

"Other than the main characters, sometimes it's hard to know, so all I can do is guess. Peter will either be the werewolf in wolf form for the first chapter, or Thorne, the other vampire hunter. I'm not sure if I'll not show up or be cast in a male role. Normally, I'd be the wolf handler, but she's not in this scene. This will be an interesting experiment," Bobbie enthused.

Rolling my eyes, I took the book from her and turned it over. The cover was matte black and a blurb on the back told about the story. I was careful not to read any of it, lest we be pulled into the plot before we were ready. There was still much about the legacy magic we didn't understand, most of which we were learning the hard way. Every. Time.

The front listed the title and author's name, Hillary Shannon, along with the moon in the background, taking up most of the cover. On the bottom left portion of the cover a wolf silhouette howled at the moon opposite the silhouettes of two people running. I couldn't really judge the book by its cover, I didn't have anything to compare it with. I assumed it was pretty normal for this type of genre.

I did look up Hillary Shannon, but she hadn't published anything else and didn't even have an author web page. Maybe she was some kind of dark horse like the sparkly vampire author, and *Chase the Night* will end up being some kind of phenomenon. After this, I think I'll be pretty qualified to give her a review.

"Are we ready, then?" Bobbie asked.

"As I'll ever be. Here goes," I cracked the spine and turned to page one.

Chase the Night

Stacia closely followed Thorne into the cave. The wolf leading them stayed several yards ahead. The waves crashing behind them faded as they rounded corner after corner until only the sound of their footsteps and soft breaths remained.

The wolf slowed and Thorne did as well, raising his hand to keep Stacia behind him. He pulled his dagger from its sheath. This wasn't just any dagger. The Hunter's dagger, passed to Thorne from his father, and his father before him. Carved from a solid piece of hornbeam, the wood had been honed as sharp as any metal blade. It was oiled and cared for like a steel blade as well, and it never failed. The patina gleamed, picking up and reflecting the faint light from Stacia's flashlight. Had it been daylight, you could have seen the stain of ancient blood on the blade.

"You must be far enough away that your prey cannot

sense you, yet close enough to move in before the *were* loses control and tears the parasite to bits. 'Tis its nature. If the werewolf draws blood, even we won't be able to stop it," Thorne softly instructed Stacia.

"I may be a novice, but I'm not an imbecile," she retorted in a whisper. "I know the shifter's nature from my first year of training." The species, which could change from human to animal form, preferred to be called *shifters*, but old-school Thorne continued to call them werewolves, or simply *weres*. He was too arrogant to care about being politically correct, despite the invaluable assistance they provided Hunters.

Thorne glared at her in the weak light. He relished his role as instructor, the responsibility of imparting his vast wealth of knowledge to new Hunters. Had he married, he would be training his own son or daughter by now. Their demand so high, fewer Hunters were taking the time to start families of their own. With fewer Hunters by bloodline available, it was important that the knowledge and skills be passed to recruits thoroughly and precisely.

Ignoring her comment, Thorne focused his attention back to the wolf, who stopped, but stood on alert. Its stance indicated that it was safe to approach, for now. Stacia turned on her watch; in fifteen minutes the sun would set. They were safe for the time being but would have to hurry. This vampire was old, and wily. It was very possible that the darkness of the caves allowed it to waken earlier than younger demons.

"Xavier, we must take him alive. We must discover how far his network extends and we can't do that if he's dead," Thorne spoke to the wolf, who responded with a low, irritated growl.

Stacia wanted to reach out and stroke the beast's fluffy neck but knew it would be unprofessional and unappreciated; he wasn't a dog, after all, or even a wolf most of the time.

"Come," Thorne said softly.

Stacia tightened her grip on the kit bag and followed. This was the most dangerous thing a Hunter could do, surprise a vampire in its lair. A vampire was most vulnerable during the day when it slept. The Hunters planned to get in and incapacitate it before it woke. Usually, a lair would be protected by traps or the vampire's drudge, but this vamp was known to be a loner. It protected itself by constantly moving. Thorne had been tracking it for years.

Stacia felt defenseless with her hands occupied by the flashlight and kit. She trusted Thorne and his experience to keep her safe. Thorne moved forward; the wolf stayed at her side. He was here for protection as well as tracking. Stacia shined her light ahead so Thorne could see and carefully followed.

After several more turns the passage opened into a giant cavern. Once carved out by the ocean, the waves hadn't reached this far back in centuries and the rocks littering the floor were remarkably dry. Perfect for a vampire nap.

Thorne reached back and took the flashlight from Stacia's hand. He swept it slowly around the cavern, starting low and working his way up. The space looked to be one hundred feet wide and perhaps forty in depth. Falling rocks reshaped the perimeter, which had probably not been smooth to begin with.

The shadows hung deep beyond Thorne's moving light. There were too many places a vampire could tuck itself away. While the Hunter searched with his eyes, Xavier tested the air. He padded next to Thorne and nudged him to the left. Thorne concentrated in that direction, taking cautious steps forward, following the wolf. Stacia hung back. She silently unzipped the kit and pulled out the banded steel restraints, taking care they didn't clank. Thorne and the wolf rounded a stone formation the size of a truck and disappeared from view. Suddenly the silent cavern echoed with sounds of scuffling, hissing, and growls.

"Stacia, to me!" Thorne shouted.

Penny grabbed the kit and hurried to her mentor. Without killing it, they wouldn't be able to hold the vamp for long. She rounded the rocks and found the vamp on his knees. Thorne stood behind him with blade poised at his quarry's pale neck. His face was flushed from exertion and a lock of graying hair now brushed the cheekbone below one penetrating blue eye. His biceps bulged, straining to hold his quarry. The wolf stood, teeth bared, with his claws digging into the vampire's impressive chest.

The vampire, rather than looking angry, had a bemused expression on its face. Tripp tensed when his prisoner reached into its own mouth and prodded at the elongated canines protruding from its gums.

"Duuuude, fangs!"

"Peter?!" I asked. *What the heck happened?*

****

"Penny?" Tripp removed the knife from Peter's neck and shook his hair out of his face.

"I thought you were supposed to be the vampire." I looked from Tripp to the wolf. "Bobbie?" The wolf just continued to growl at Peter.

"Hey, Fido, chill with the claws, would ya?" Peter attempted to remove the giant paws pressing into his chest.

"I take it this isn't going quite as planned," Tripp said. He sheathed his blade and bent to help Peter with his wolf problem. The wolf allowed it this time, then sat down with its tongue lolling out of its mouth.

"Bobbie!" I called, because the Bobbie I knew would never let her tongue hang like that.

"Penny!"

I looked around. Tripp peered at the ceiling, trying to locate Bobbie. Peter was trying out his new vampire-fast ninja moves. I ignored his nonchalance regarding his missing girlfriend.

"Where are you?" I called, my voice echoing through the cavern.

"I…I don't know. I don't think I'm anywhere, but I can see you and I can see the words on the pages of the book…oh, no," Bobbie's voice groaned, "I'm the narrator!"

"Say what?"

"I'm the narrator; I read everything that isn't dialogue, like an audio book, but with the characters having their own speaking parts."

"That's never happened before," Tripp and I said at the same time. We were both peering up, as if that's where Bobbie's disembodied voice came from. Peter stopped his ninja imitation and went back to poking at his fangs.

"How?" Tripp asked.

"I'm not sure…," Bobbie answered hesitantly. I sensed evasion.

"And I thought you said Tripp would be the

vampire, the main character and love interest. How's that supposed to work now? I'll have scenes with Peter instead. No offense, but eww."

"None taken, Penn. You're like my sister or something," Peter added, though clearly not as disturbed by the series of events as Tripp and me.

"So if I'm this Thorne guy, what's my role?" Tripp asked, moving closer to me, but keeping an eye on the wolf, who sat scratching its unmentionables.

"Let me think for a minute," Bobbie pleaded.

"Babe," Peter called to the ceiling. "You just need to come clean; no one will be mad. They'll be proud of you, like I am." He gave us a hard look that dared us to do otherwise.

"Argh! Peter! Fine." I'd never heard Bobbie so rattled. "Penny, I'm so sorry, I should have told you, but I'm Hillary Shannon."

Tripp sent me a questioning look.

"The author?" I asked, trying to wrap my brain around what she was saying.

"Yes, I'm the author. I had no idea any of this would happen. I think because I wrote the story, the magic cast me as the narrator. And I guess since I created the main character with my own personal love interest in mind, Peter got cast as the vampire."

Tripp held up his hands. "Whoa, whoa, hold up. How did you write and get this published so fast? We've only been doing this a few months."

"Bobbie's been writing for a long time. Last year I finally talked her into publishing some of it." Peter's chest puffed with pride.

"How come you never told me? This is kind of a big deal." I couldn't believe she hadn't shared this with me.

She was my best friend—she knew all about my family curse and everything. It hurt.

"I'm sorry Penny; so, so sorry. I didn't mean to keep it from you, but my writing is fluff. I'm having trouble being proud of the accomplishment while being embarrassed by the content. It's not even the kind of thing I enjoy reading. I tried a couple different light fiction genres to help me relax, but some of the plots were so ridiculous, I couldn't focus. I started writing because I felt like it wouldn't be hard to do a better job. Eventually, instead of reading, I found myself writing romantic fiction to relax."

"So the whole bit about you reading this book and loving it was all a lie?"

I could sense her cringing even if I couldn't see her. "It's the one I thought was good enough to publish."

"How much of that decision has to do with my situation?" I asked. Tripp was right; we hadn't been dealing with the legacy long enough for Bobbie to have created a whole story for me.

"I've had this one written for a little over a year now. Once we figured out what you were dealing with, I started the publishing process. I'd honestly hoped it would provide us with more control."

Tripp snorted.

"I am proud of you. It's very cool that you've published a book. I'm just shocked." I gave Tripp a reproachful look.

"So, madam narrator, what do we need to do to finish out this scene?" Tripp asked, trying, almost successfully, to mask the annoyance in his voice. His irritated expression gave him away, though.

"Um, the vampire, Lucien, and Stacia lock eyes and

make a connection. You, Thorne, restrain him and escort him to the Hunters' containment headquarters."

I glanced at Peter, currently trying to crush a rock in the palm of his hand. "Gotcha," I said. "But that first part isn't going to happen."

"All right, let's go." Tripp shined the light in the direction we'd come from and stalked off. The rest of us could follow or stand around in the dark. The wolf trailed behind, occasionally nipping at Peter's heels.

I caught up to Tripp and snagged his empty hand in mine. "I'll call you tonight, okay?"

"Sure," he said shortly, but let go of my hand to wrap his arm around my shoulders. He squeezed me and kissed the top of my head. This was an unusual turn of events, in already, beyond unusual circumstances. All we could do was roll with it.

Chapter 2

Oh, What a Tangled Web

I glared at Bobbie from my seat in the reading nook, my favored read-in location when bringing guests. She had the grace to look sheepish; Peter immediately went to stand behind her chair, placing a supportive (or possibly protective) hand on her shoulder.

"I'm not mad," I said. "I'm disappointed."

"You sound like my mom." Peter frowned at me.

"Well, it's true. I'm disappointed you didn't feel you could share it with me," I clarified. "This family legacy is the biggest thing in my life, other than this bookstore, and I've shared every bit of both those things with you."

"But those are things that have happened to you. This is something I've created. It was hard to release it into the world. I wanted to tell you so many times. Then I told myself, if you read it, you'd only tell me what I wanted to hear. This way, using it as the read-in book, I decided you'd be able to give me your unbiased feedback. If you hated it, I'd never have to tell you I wrote it. It was a cowardly mistake; I realize that now." She gave me a self-conscious half-smile. "I was a little enamored with the idea of being inside my own creation; how many authors get to do that? I'm sorry. I've used your problem for my own gain, and that was so wrong. Please forgive me?" Her eyes pleaded with me, and Peter raised his brows, encouraging me to get on with it.

I moved to the chair Peter vacated and pulled Bobbie's hands into mine. "Of course, you're forgiven. For the record, if I'd known you wrote a book, I would have insisted using it for this." I squeezed her hands gently. "But it isn't working out the way you intended, is it?" I thought back to Tripp's character, the aging hunter with his graying hair.

"No, I'm so sorry. What a mess! I don't even know how it's going to work now with Tripp cast as the bad guy."

In the last two books, Peter, his Aunt Biddy, my neighbor Gregorio, and Tripp's sister had all been read-in to non-essential roles. The only one to show up as a non-essential in the same book twice was Gregorio, but he returned as the same character. I suspected the cast list was set and Peter would have to continue being a vampire. Poor Tripp.

"You're like, the writer and the narrator, right?" Peter asked. "Couldn't you like, change it as we go?"

Bobbie and I looked at each other, both surprised by the idea and that Peter thought of it. He was a history guy, not a language arts buff.

"I don't know. Maybe we could test it out next time. I'll rewrite some of it. I'll need to change Stacia's love interest, rearrange the plot, and create more scenes with Stacia and Thorne," Bobbie said, the wheels already turning.

"I can email the new pages to Tripp for when he reads-in." I glanced at my watch. "I need to go call him and explain things. If the plot manipulation doesn't work, maybe it will be enough to convince him to finally meet in person." I got up and gave both Bobbie and Peter a hug, then headed upstairs, trusting them to lock up when they left.

****

"Hey," I said tentatively, when Tripp answered the phone.

"Hey," he returned, sounding more than slightly disgruntled.

I jumped right in. "Bobbie's really sorry."

"Penny, I'm old, and also, not a vampire, though I don't know yet if that's good or bad."

"But you were a totally sexy older man. You know, guys get hotter when they get older. It's one of those unfair laws of nature." I could almost hear him frowning.

"How badly is this going to mess up what we're trying to accomplish?" he asked.

"Well, we're hoping that since Bobbie is the author and narrator, maybe she can shift the plot. Obviously, this isn't anything any of the grandmothers have encountered, so we're flying a bit blind. We're not sure what the magic will allow."

"You said before, so long as our actions seemed to be for the betterment of progressing the relationship, the magic would give us leeway."

"Let's hope this falls under the allowable category. Changing the plot will certainly be pressing the boundaries," I said. This would be more than simply going off-script for a bit to chat. This would be more like script-jacking. "We could always meet in real life and be done with the books." I didn't mention that we'd still be unable to read a regular book until after we were married. The idea still freaked me out. We were definitely connecting, and our chemistry was undeniable, but that didn't necessarily make for a lifelong commitment. I knew he wasn't on board yet either.

"No," he said abruptly. "We can try Bobbie's rewrite, and if that doesn't work we'll make do. Even old, I'm still a badass vampire Hunter," he said with, I imagined, a sexy grin.

"The baddest," I agreed.

"Kaitlyn wants to come again. She's a big fan of those kinds of books. When I mentioned it, she was pretty excited. My copy should be here in the next couple days."

"I'll tell Bobbie. She might have an easier time manipulating the plot if the characters are willing to follow her lead. Otherwise, the characters may tend to stay on script while we're all going another direction."

"Sounds like a plausible theory. What characters are left? The wolf?"

"Yes, but, he's a boy. There's also the wolf handler. She's a wolf too but doesn't shift or something like that. She's got some kind of connection so he can talk to her when he's in wolf form. I don't remember the details though. Most likely, Kaitlyn would be that character since she's a girl."

"So that leaves an unpredictable animal as the last character? Brilliant. I'm sure nothing will go wrong," Tripp said sarcastically. "I won't put Kaitlyn in danger."

"I'll see what Bobbie has to say, okay?" Actually, I had an idea, but Tripp wasn't going to like it, not one bit.

Chapter 3

Way More Mr. Nice Guy

Thursday morning found me at the shop. Bobbie would be in around one, so I would discuss my ideas and Kaitlyn then. I'd finally purchased a couple of half whiskey barrel planters for the shop's front entrance. I didn't particularly have a green thumb, but I'd helped my mom with the flower beds when I was younger, how hard could it be? Besides, it wasn't like I actually had to grow anything from seed. The nursery provided me with dirt and two flats of marigolds, which they assured me were very hearty so long as I remembered to water them.

I temporarily parked in front of the shop to unload. I rolled the barrels out of the back seat and unloaded the flats from the trunk. I stared at the two forty-pound bags of potting soil resting in my trunk. I worked out... sometimes; I could lift the weight. The angle gave me pause, though. I would have to bend, reach forward, then lift to get them out, all while balancing on the curb.

"Do you need help?" A voice behind me asked.

"Gregorio!" I turned and gave him a quick hug. "Your timing is perfect. Would you mind lifting these out of my trunk?" I stepped aside so he could get to the trunk.

"Of course not. If you put your planters where you want them, I'll empty them in for you," he offered.

15

"That would be awesome. Thanks." I quickly moved the barrels to flank the front door and moved the flats so Gregorio wouldn't step on them. He made quick and clean work of emptying the bags, a project that would undoubtedly have ended with dirt on me and on the sidewalk if I attempted it myself.

Before he could say his goodbyes and walk away, I decided to broach the subject that had been on my mind all morning. Since I should really talk to Bobbie first, I wouldn't go into a lot of detail with Gregorio. I considered it more of a fact-finding mission.

Gregorio brushed his mostly still clean hands off on his cargo shorts. I found it barely warm enough for that kind of attire, but then again, I didn't spend my days working construction or lifting dirt out of people's trunks.

"So, we started another book last night," I began.

He focused his golden hazel eyes on mine. "Really? And how did that go?"

"We had a bit of a problem, actually. Nobody except me ended up in the parts we were supposed to."

"Tripp was not your main character's love interest? How did that happen?"

"Funny thing. Turns out, Bobbie literally wrote the book we're reading, though we didn't know it beforehand. Since Peter is her love interest in real life, he ended up as the main character. Bobbie was the narrator, so we could hear her, but not see her."

"Tripp couldn't have been happy about that turn of events," Gregorio smirked. "What are you going to do?"

"Bobbie is going to try to turn the story."

"What character did Tripp play? What is the story about this time?"

"I think his character is the antagonist, the bad guy. The story is actually a paranormal romance, if you can believe that."

Gregorio laughed out loud. "I cannot imagine Bobbie writing such a thing, but I do not know her well. After being cast the villain in both of your other stories, I am gratified Tripp will now also be able to experience the frustration." His eyes twinkled and he wore the biggest smile on his face. "This I would like to see."

"Really? You'd go back into one of my stories?" I was leading here, but when I presented my idea to Bobbie, I wanted to be able to tell her Gregorio would help.

"Penelope, the first time was horrifying because of what the scene entailed." Poor guy, he would never get over assaulting me, even though he couldn't control any of his actions at the time. "The second time I quite enjoyed. I sort of knew what was happening and the character was not really evil." He'd rocked the sexy, greaser bad boy persona, definitely not evil. "I would not mind participating again. It's a once in a lifetime experience, is it not? But I don't think Tripp would like it."

Though, not my goal, I suspected that would actually be a selling point for him, antagonizing Tripp. The two men established an instant dislike for each other based on testosterone-fueled misplaced jealousy.

"I need to talk to Bobbie about it, but there's a possibility we might need all the characters filled in order to turn the plot." So much for fact finding. I was really bad keeping my cards close to my vest.

"What part would I play?" he asked hesitantly.

"Most likely the werewolf. It's the only male part

17

left. Bobbie needs to turn the story, to make Tripp my love interest instead of Peter." Eww.

Gregorio laughed again. "Yes, I can see that she would want to do that. A werewolf, huh? That would certainly be a unique experience."

"It's a romance, so I don't think you'd have to rip anybody's throat out or any horror movie stuff like that."

He gave me a stern look. "Please find out, Penelope. That would be a deal breaker. But it would be nice to participate as an invited guest rather than a surprise interloper."

"I'm going to talk to Bobbie about it this afternoon. I'll text you and let you know what she says. We're hoping to do another reading on Friday night."

"I'll make sure I'm free. I originally stopped by to let you know Cora will be moving into the apartment in three weeks. Everything should be ready by then."

"That's great news. Though it does put my relationship with Tripp on a bit of a deadline. We won't be able to read-in with Cora living next door. That's OK, we'll make it work." I smiled at him. Time was getting short. A little thrill shot through me. I'd get to meet Tripp in person within the next two weeks. I grinned as I dug my fingers into the warm soil and started transplanting marigolds.

Chapter 4

I Can't Foresee Any Problems With This Plan

"Hey, Tripometer, I brought your mail." Kaitlyn pranced into the shop. There were a few customers milling around. A guy checking out my selection of holsters glanced over, then gave Kaitlyn a second, slower perusal. I caught his eye and gave him a dark look; he moved on to another section of the store. I knew guys considered Kaitlyn pretty. But she was twenty-three, and *I* still considered her a kid. She wasn't available to anyone who hadn't been thoroughly vetted.

I inputted inventory off invoices while watching the front counter. Scott wasn't due until one. "Wow, thanks. That will save me having to open the mailbox as I walk right by it on the way up to my door." When I moved into my parent's property, I'd applied for my own address. I'm not suggesting my mom is nosey, she didn't mean to be, but my time in the service made me covet any bit of privacy available to me. Besides, someday I'd move out and they'd have a real renter who would insist on separate addresses.

"I know! Aren't I a great sister? It's just some bills, and oh, what's this?" It's really fortunate she didn't decide to pursue acting. "Tripp, it looks like your book came." I took the package from her, surprised that it hadn't mysteriously been torn open on her way here. I

19

did the honors and pulled my fresh copy of *Chase the Night* out of the padded envelope. Kaitlyn wound her fingers together to keep from grabbing the book out of my hands, but she couldn't keep herself from bouncing on her toes in anticipation.

"Well, are you going to open it?"

I lowered my voice. "I really don't dare. I don't want to end up in it right now. There were some problems with the first read-in. Penny needs to discuss some things with Bobbie before we go in again. But good news for you, there is a possibility they will need you for a character on a permanent basis."

"Eeee!" she squealed. "That would be awesome. Can I?" She held her hand out for the book. I gave it over and she read the synopsis on the back, then studied the front cover. "I could read it though, couldn't I?"

"I suppose, but hopefully it's all going to change." She gave me a puzzled look. "Hillary Shannon," I pointed to the authors name on the cover, "is really Penny's friend, Bobbie."

"No way! That's cool."

"Actually, not really, 'cause it really messed up our first read-in. Bobbie was put in position of narrator and her boyfriend, Peter, ended up in the lead spot. It slotted me as the bad guy. We're hoping, that since Bobbie is the author and narrator, she'll be able to change the story from within. Penny and I thought that might be easier if all the characters were people she knew."

Kaitlyn contemplated this for a moment, then carefully opened the book to the first chapter. "Stacia followed closely behind Thorne…"

"Stop! I don't even know if I can hear it read out loud without something happening, so just don't, OK?"

"Geez, don't get your panties in a bunch." She scanned the page then fanned through to the end. Only one hundred twenty-eight pages. This is really more novella length."

"What?"

"It's not long enough to be considered a full novel. This length is referred to as a novella. It's great for people not able to commit to a longer story or with short attention spans."

"Humph. Commitment phobes and millennials, sounds right up your alley, Sis."

She gave me a dirty look and a shrug. "Good for busy people too. So can I?"

"Can you what?"

"Take it with me to read this afternoon."

I started to reach across the counter but caught myself. Kaitlyn would take good care of it. She may act flighty, but sometimes it really was just an act. I clenched my fist at my side. "Sure. Do me a favor, though, would you?" She cocked her head, waiting for my condition. "Read it at my place."

She leaned over and kissed my cheek. "Of course. If I go home, mom will find a chore for me to do anyway. I'll tell her you paid me to clean." I brightened and she laughed. "Not a chance. I'd never meet your standards anyway, Sergeant." She picked up the rest of my mail from the counter and stuffed it and the book back into the padded envelope. She then tucked the works into her oversized purse. "I'll see you later?"

"I'll be home a little after five. Tell you what, I'll bring home pizza and you can tell me all about the story over dinner."

"Make it a deep-dish double pepperoni and it's a

deal."

I agreed and Kaitlyn sauntered out, as buoyantly as she'd arrived.

Chapter 5

Pants on Fire

I stared at my phone. I could only put off this conversation for so long before my actions were deemed a sin of omission.

Bobbie had been excited about the idea of filling all the character slots and appreciative of Gregorio's willingness to help us out. She was skeptical about his motives, though.

Gregorio and I went out a few times and he had been interested in pursuing a relationship. I agreed, at first, until things with Tripp started becoming more serious. We parted friends with no hard feelings. Bobbie was friendly with Gregorio but firmly on 'Team Tripp' in regards to me. Her concern wasn't completely unfounded. He and Tripp behaved like dogs fighting over a bone, or bonehead in this case. I couldn't figure out a way to stifle or resolve their immature animosity.

I don't know how Gregorio felt about me, but his over-protectiveness suggested Bobbie might be right. He was keeping his options open in case things with Tripp and me didn't work out.

He was an attractive guy, for sure, but a few weeks ago I discovered he was my gazillion-times-removed cousin, or something like that. The information succeeded in firmly pushing him into the 'friend zone' portion of my brain. Now, I didn't view him as anything more than a dear friend, or possibly a brother.

I, of course, hadn't shared my discoveries with him yet. I worried he'd see the connection as an argument in favor of a relationship rather than against since no government would ever consider us related.

I hadn't told Tripp about it either, or about the actual extent of my research into the possible true love options of my many-greats grandmother, Elizabeth. For one, I didn't want him to think I was actively looking for a back-door solution to ending the curse while we were getting along so well. Secondly, I didn't need him making wrong assumptions about Gregorio and me.

It also never turned out well when I mentioned Gregorio in Tripp's presence. He hated the guy. Which brought me back to the dreaded phone call I needed to make.

"I think it'd be great to have Gregorio help, but you know, you have to tell Tripp," Bobbie said, when I told her my idea yesterday.

I gritted my teeth. "But why? He's been in before. I know they don't get along but…" I hadn't really thought that argument out very well.

"Because there are too many people involved and it *will* come to light that Gregorio's presence was planned, then you will be in big trouble. I don't want to have to narrate around Tripp's temper tantrum. I need this to go smoothly, so we can gauge if it will even work. Everyone needs to play their parts. Besides," she continued, "you don't want to start a relationship with lies between you."

I grabbed the phone and pressed three on the speed dial before I could change my mind. "Penny, is everything okay? Are we still reading tonight?" Tripp asked when he answered the phone. "The pages you sent are all printed and ready to go."

"Yes, everything is fine. I needed to talk to you about something first. Bobbie thought it would be a good idea to fill all the character slots with our own people to ensure that the new pages come off without a hitch." Totally true. "Um, you see, Gregorio offered to help us with the wolf character." Also, technically true.

"Really? And how did Gregorio even find out about any of it?" Busted.

"It came up in conversation." Not a lie.

"Humph. I thought you said he found a renter for the space next door. Why is he still around so much?"

"His renter moves in a couple weeks. He's still finishing up. I know you don't like him, but he's a friend to me."

"Oh, I'm sure he'd like to be more."

"Maybe so, but he's a very upstanding guy. He knows he's in the friend zone and won't do anything to jeopardize that," I said in Gregorio's defense.

"I feel like he's hanging around waiting for me to fail," Tripp said in a rare moment of vulnerability. My heart swelled and turned mushy. "Isn't there anyone else you can use?"

"The only other person who knows about the legacy is Peter's grandmother, Aunt Biddy. She's as liable to hijack the plot as she is to help. Besides, I can't really see her in the male wolf part. It might not even work." I needed to address Tripp's other comments. "It's not a contest you know, Gregorio isn't some kind of backup plan. My heart already knows you. This getting to know each other that we're doing, it's only a formality to satisfy our modern sensibilities. Our relationship is a crazy cross between love at first sight and an arranged marriage. Neither of which is currently in fashion. But know this, no matter what happens, it's you." It was kind of deep in the feels for a phone declaration, but I didn't think I would have the nerve to say it to his face. I blushed thinking about him on the other end of the line.

"Thank you for that," he said gruffly. "I'll try to lay off Gregorio tonight. How much trouble can he possibly be as a dog anyway?"

Chapter 6

Here Goes Nothing

I emerged from the bedroom and returned to the kitchen where Kaitlyn was putting away dinner leftovers.

"Everything okay?" She furrowed her brow.

I never got calls from girls let alone ones that sent me shuffling off to the bedroom for privacy. This was new territory for both of us. "Yeah, everything's fine. Penny wanted to warn me Gregorio would be there tonight playing the part of the wolf."

Her brow remained pinched. "Wasn't he that guy who was picking on you?" Sibling protectiveness at its finest.

I snorted. "Hardly. We don't get along. Period. You make it sound like I can't take care of myself."

She opened her mouth to respond but snapped it closed.

"I am perfectly capable both there and here."

"Well, I thought he was a jerk. What's his deal, anyway?"

I looked at the kitchen clock. We only had a few minutes before we needed to read. "He owns the building next to Penny. They dated very briefly. He probably still has a thing for her." Who wouldn't? "Have you looked over the new pages?" I asked, changing the subject.

"Yes, the story is basically the same except now it's

my character that gets kidnapped. There's no romance with the vampire, at least not yet, and you're looking good as the hero so far." She smirked. "But you're still old."

I ignored her jab. "Sounds good. Let's go sit in the living room." I grabbed sodas for both of us and Kaitlyn grabbed a fudgsicle from the freezer. I purchased them for her anyway. I told her what Penny said about her coffee still being hot when she'd returned from a read-in, even though it felt like she'd been gone for hours. Kaitlyn mentioned testing the theory with cold items. We settled into the sofa and recliner. I couldn't get comfortable, like someone told me to 'act natural', guaranteeing that I would be able to do anything but.

Kaitlyn twisted the cap off her drink and took a swallow. She placed her still-wrapped treat directly on the coffee table. I gave her a look and she shrugged. The book and new pages were already resting on the table. She slid the loose pages over to me. I picked them up and pushed my chair into the reclined position, placing my own drink into the armrest cup holder. Ah, bachelor living. I straightened the pages in my hands and began, "Chapter two…"

Chase the Night

The trio climbed up the side of the cliff using the ropes left from their descent earlier that evening. The hunters secured themselves with the lines, forcing the restrained vampire to rely on its preternatural agility and immortality should it fall. A single rope around its waist, tethered it to Thorne. The wolf trailed well behind to intercept the vampire should it attempt escape. Once the Hunters and their prisoner neared the top, the wolf bounded up behind them using a narrow fox trail and its supernatural balancing skills.

They were met at the top by the fourth member of their team, Crystal, Xavier's mate. Not able to shift into wolf form herself, she maintained a telepathic connection to him in both his forms. While the connection was strong, it could be strained or disrupted by distance or earth formations, such as caves. Crystal grabbed Stacia's hand and helped her over the precipice.

Thorne launched himself up and over like a man half his age, making Stacia wonder if anything short of death would force his retirement. Thorne pulled on the rope at his waist, half dragging the vampire up behind him. The wolf closed-in, making the vamp aware of his presence. This was a critical point in the capture. The vampire was strong enough to throw Thorne or Stacia back over the edge of the cliff. Only sure dismemberment by werewolf, kept it in check.

Crystal retrieved additional restraints from the van and moved to secure the vampire's legs. The wolf crowded in, growling, and she gave him a little shove with her hip. "Knock it off, Xavier. Let me do my job."

"Your pet, he does not like me much. No?" The vampire chuckled.

Xavier placed his teeth around one of the vampire's ankles and applied pressure.

The vampire chuckled again. "If your master wanted me dead, I would be so already."

Thorne cut in. "I need you alive for now, but not necessarily with all your limbs. Quit provoking my *were*, parasite."

Both Crystal and her mate flicked annoyed glares at Thorne, but quickly finished securing the vampire.

Thorne laid a firm hand on the vampire's shoulder

and shoved him toward the waiting van. "Lucien DeFrost. You are under the jurisdiction of The Alliance for the Control of Unnatural Populations. Understand that the only outcome of this seizure will be your death. However, the quality of your remaining existence can be improved by your cooperation."

The vampire, Lucien, sneered. "I know who you are Thorne, and to whom you grovel. I am not, however, familiar with your pretty assistants."

Both Crystal and Stacia stiffened, and the wolf crowded in again, dogging Lucien's heels all the way to the van.

"They are unimportant to your situation." Thorne shackled Lucien to heavy duty chains welded into the van. The wolf clambered in behind and Thorne slammed the door. He turned to Crystal "Take Stacia and follow me. The vampire has taken an interest in both of you, and I don't want her in the van." He then strode to the vehicle, climbed in, and sped off without a backward glance.

"What a jerk!" Crystal said.

"Mmm," Stacia agreed absently, savoring the memory of Thorne's powerful stride and authoritative demeanor.

"Whoa, whoa, whoa! What?" Crystal asked. "Does she not even have enough self-respect to know that guy's a misogynistic creep? I know he's my brother and all, and not really like that, but if Stacia is going to have to put up with that attitude for the rest of the book, I'm probably going to murder him."

Penny placed her hand on Kaitlyn's arm. "It's okay. I'm sure Bobbie has a plan. I assume it's not easy to turn a plot."

Bobbie's disembodied voice encompassed them. "I can't just make a U-turn; I have to gradually turn the plot. Thorne's personality has already been firmly established. I'm afraid the magic would rebel if I changed him all at once. Step one: Thorne shows aloof concern at the vampire's interest in Stacia."

"Okay, okay," Kaitlyn conceded. "Guys who act like that piss me off."

"Me too." I tentatively put my arm around her shoulders. "What's next?" I asked Bobbie. Once again, her voice surrounded us. "Follow the van. From what I can see, the road ends where you are. So take it back the other direction till you see where the van ended up."

"Do you want to drive?" I asked Kaitlyn. We both turned to check out our ride. "Technically, it's probably yours since I would have ridden with Thorne, er, Tripp."

She whistled through her teeth. A skill I envied. "Looks like being a werewolf vampire hunter pays pretty well. I'll definitely drive." Parked beside the road sat a sleek, super sporty black Jaguar. It was a two-seater, so definitely not used for transporting vampires. I wondered if the irony of two wolves owning a car named after a cat was intentional. Bobbie wrote it, so no doubt it was.

Kaitlyn rounded to the driver's side, and I threw my vampire capturing kit bag in the trunk. When I got into the passenger seat, Kaitlyn was caressing the car's wheel and dashboard in awe.

"Let's go. I don't want to be too far behind them." I pulled the door shut.

She started the engine. It gave a throaty roar, then settled into a hearty purr. After a few lurches and fishtails Kaitlyn got control the vehicle, and we took off down the road a little faster than I would have liked.

"So, that was really weird back there. Your friend, the wolf guy, I could hear his voice in my head. Like, I could hear him threatening the vampire and grousing at Tripp, well, at Thorne." She hesitated. "I guess he would have fussed at either of them, huh?"

"My wolf friend is Gregorio, he's really a nice guy. He and Tripp just don't see eye to eye." I decided to steer the topic someplace safer. "I can't believe Bobbie actually named the hunter organization A-CUP."

Kaitlyn snorted, much like I'd seen Tripp do. "I guess we can assume we won't be using the acronym for our little organization." She gave me a half-smile, but kept her eyes on the road. "So anyway," she was obviously not going to be sidetracked. "The wolf…Gregorio, what's the deal? Tripp said you used to date. Isn't that weird to still be friends and hang out?"

"We went out twice. You couldn't really consider it dating, it wasn't like that. I met him when his uncle, my previous neighbor, died. We didn't start out as friends then date. We just went out." Argh! I was over-explaining this so much. "I essentially met Gregorio and Tripp around the same time. The thing with Tripp is a lot more involved and it wouldn't have been fair of me to date outside of that situation. So I stopped dating, I mean, I didn't go out with Gregorio again. But he *is* a nice guy. I would totally recommend him if you're interested."

"Uh. No. The first time I met him he was picking on my brother, and now he's a dog. No thank you. I'm not desperate, you know."

I didn't assume that at all. She was cute and blonde and spunky, the triumvirate of attractiveness. At least I'd succeeded in getting her to drop the subject of Gregorio.

The sun set and twilight settled in. I couldn't see

much out my window, but I don't think I missed anything important. No roads split off from ours and there were no buildings on our route. I worried about the story happening without us. I hoped everyone was getting along.

Chapter 7

PG-13

Chase the Night

I coaxed more speed out of the van, conscious of Peter the vampire chained up in the back. That had to be uncomfortable. I could hear him attempting to chat with Gregorio, who was obviously, unable to respond. I didn't mind Penny's neighbor so much when I didn't have to look at him or hear him.

"How much further, Papa Smurf?" Peter called from the back.

"The road dead ended at a warehouse that backed up to the forest," Bobbie narrated. Her voice now seemed to be issuing from the radio speaker.

"Thanks, Bobbie," I said, as the warehouse became visible in my headlights.

The wolf, Gregorio, appeared next to me, his back legs crouched, then he launched himself into the passenger seat.

"That's not really the safest place for you without a seat belt," I said. The wolf gave me a side eye. "Next time I'll see if I can find a crate for you," I added with a grin. This time he didn't look at me, but his lip curled, and a low rumble escaped his throat.

I turned into the warehouse driveway, faster than necessary, apologizing silently to Peter in the back.

Gregorio managed to stay upright, but barely. I winced when claws on all four of his paws pierced the leather seats. Bobbie's attention to detail was impressive. This was quite a state-of-the-art vampire catching van. I put the van in park and jumped out slamming the door behind me. Mr. No-Opposable Thumbs could climb out the back the same way he got in.

I opened the rear and pulled the keys to the chains out of my pocket. Peter looked relaxed, despite the rough ride and rougher accommodations. But, from my experience, the guy didn't get worked up about much.

As I leaned in to deal with the locks, the wolf shoved past me on his way out the doors. Jerk. He bounced over to the warehouse and placed his front paws on the door. When it didn't budge, he stepped back a few paces and sat down in what appeared to be a sulk. I'm pretty sure he regretted agreeing to this.

"Probably need the keys, pal." I helped Peter out of the van. "Here, why don't you go ahead and open up for us." I tossed him the keys, which he attempted to catch in the most YouTube-worthy fashion I'd ever seen.

Having not been born a wolf, Gregorio had none of the wolf's natural reflexes. I could see his brain work as he first attempted to grab the keys out of the air with his paws. He looked like a cat preparing to catch a moth in the air. At the last minute, he must have realized as a canine, he should catch them in his mouth, but by then it was too late. Paws up and mouth open, the keys smacked him on the end of his nose fairly hard, then dropped to the ground. Gregorio flinched, which threw him off balance. He twisted and fell awkwardly onto his back. He righted himself, then literally formed the downward facing dog yoga pose and put his paws over his nose with a whine.

My conscience tweaked a tiny bit. I was normally against animal cruelty. "Sorry, bro. Did you forget you wouldn't be able to use them anyway?"

"Tripp, not cool man, you totally booped him on the nose," Peter scolded almost with a straight face. At that point, we both busted out laughing. "Sorry, my friend," Peter addressed Gregorio. "But you should have seen yourself, man."

The wolf sat up, sniffed, sneezed, and proceeded to glare at us, which may have been chilling had we not just witnessed his humiliation, not to mention the wolfy sneeze. This caused Peter and I to break into a second round of hilarity. He stood and padded to where the keys lay on the ground. Still maintaining eye contact with us, he slowly lifted his back leg. Peter and I sobered quickly.

"Really, not cool, man."

"Don't even think about it."

Peter and I spoke at once. We continued this standoff for several beats, before we heard the rumble of an approaching car. Gregorio dropped his leg, and Peter and I turned to see a sweet Jag pulling in behind the van. The girls emerged and came to join us. Gregorio brushed past me and pretty as you please, nuzzled Penny's hand. When she responded, he placed the keys in her palm.

"Thank you, Gregorio." She scratched behind his ear. "I thought you guys would be inside by now."

"You know I can hear you, don't you?" Kaitlyn asked sarcastically. Her hands were fisted at her hips, and she glared at Gregorio. He laid his ears flat and returned her glare with a 'ruff'. Her eyes narrowed. "I don't like you." She strode past him towards the door. "I hope this stupid place has coffee." Gregorio followed. I didn't know wolves were capable of rolling their eyes.

Penny tossed the keys to Peter, who caught them deftly. Gregorio chuffed.

"That wasn't very nice either," Kaitlyn tossed over her shoulder.

Peter unlocked the door, letting both Kaitlyn and the wolf precede him inside. He looked back at me.

"We'll be along in a minute," I said. He gave me a mock salute, and entered the building, closing the door behind him. Penny greeted me with a single lingering kiss. She stepped back and fingered the hair at my temples.

"This isn't so bad. Just enough gray to make you look distinguished." Then she trailed her fingers across my brow down my jaw line to where my shirt opened at the neck. "A hint of worry lines around your eyes."

"Those are actually mine, I'm afraid. Too much sun," I admitted.

She added her other hand and splayed her fingers across my chest, trailing them down over my abs. I sucked in a quick breath.

"Ticklish?" She twined her arms around my waist, embracing me, which I returned. "Very muscley." She hummed in approval. "Not bad at all for an old guy."

"Those are mine too." I buried my nose in her hair, enjoying the smell of mint and her.

Too soon she stepped back. "Did we miss anything?"

"Not much," I lied. "We haven't been here long."

"What do you think so far?"

"Too soon to tell. I really like Gregorio as a dog, though."

She frowned at me, so I kissed her again. She closed

her eyes and kissed me back. "I wish you'd try to get along with him," Penny mumbled against my lips.

"I am. I let him ride in the front," I replied as she pulled away.

She gave me a quelling look. I don't think she believed in the benevolence of my gesture. "Let's go in and see what Bobbie has in store for us next."

Nothing could have prepared me for what greeted us on the other side of the warehouse door. We walked into what appeared to be the lounge area of the headquarters. The floor was gray linoleum tile, and the walls were maple-colored wood paneling. To the right, was a kitchenette made up of a fridge, microwave, and peninsula. Peter stood there, shirtless, with an orange stuck in his mouth, making himself a sandwich. When we entered, he pulled the orange out of his mouth, revealing two puncture holes.

"Mystery solved," he said. "I always wondered if vampires sucked blood up through holes in their teeth like straws, or if the teeth are for making clean holes in the vein. Turns out, they're hole-makers only. Anybody else want a sandwich?"

And Peter wasn't even the strangest thing in the room. On the left wall hung heavy duty double doors that I guessed led to vampire holding cells and who knew whatever else vampire hunters might need. The room also included a battered dinette set that looked like it came from a college student's apartment. A sagging brown plaid sofa and a pair of mismatched office swivel chairs made up the supposed living room area with an old nineteen-inch TV sitting on a dusty end table. The whole place had a drug house/break room vibe. Hunters obviously spent their money on vehicles and weapons, also possibly on cool clothes I thought, tearing my eyes from the scene before me and glancing at my own expensive duds.

The scene before me, where do I start?

The question of Peter's missing shirt was answered. Gregorio, the man, the very naked man, stood behind one of the swivel chairs with Peter's shirt wrapped around his waist. For a guy usually so comfortable being an ass, he was a lot less comfortable with people seeing his ass. The term 'deer in the headlights' came to mind. I forced myself not to clamp my hand over Penny's eyes.

Kaitlyn stood across the room behind the dining table. Where Gregorio's chair of concealment intended to hide his embarrassment, Kaitlyn braced herself behind the table, as if it were armor. I didn't like Gregorio, but I was pretty sure Kaitlyn had nothing to fear from him. The expression on her face was a mix of fear, horror, and something else I couldn't put my finger on.

"What happened?" I asked.

Kaitlyn blinked and turned, noticing us for the first time. Then she blushed. Weird. "I was arguing with him." She pointed at Gregorio. "Then Bobbie's voice came out of the sky." She frantically waved her hand around in the air. "And she said something about shifting into human form, and he did. Right in front of me." She absently raked her hand through her hair, then shoved it in her pants pocket.

"It was uncomfortable on several levels," Gregorio added. His olive skin flushed as well.

"And he was naked!" Kaitlyn added unnecessarily.

"I still am." One corner of Gregorio's lips curved, causing my hackles to rise.

"But I can still hear him in my head." She yanked

her hand out of her pocket and pointed a finger at her temple.

"You are not alone in this," Gregorio told her.

"I'm so sorry, Gregorio, let me narrate you some clothes. I need to get us back on track. Everybody, hold on a minute," Bobbie's voice said from above us somewhere. I could hear her mumbling under her breath and imagined her flipping through pages trying to find where we went wrong. "Okay, sorry guys, bear with me. Here we go. 'Xavier, that's you Gregorio, exited through the double doors to find the locker room and his spare clothes.'"

"I think you're supposed to go." Penny made shooing motions when he failed to move.

With a death grip on Peter's shirt, Gregorio sidestepped to the doors, keeping his exposed thigh away from his audience. He grabbed the handle and started to pull, then stopped and looked at Kaitlyn. He smiled some kind of predatory, asshat smile that made me want to punch him in the face.

"I heard that," he said, then pulled open the door and slid through. Kaitlyn expelled her breath. Peter rushed over the door with inhuman speed, that I once again envied. He caught the door before it closed.

"Bro, my shirt." A second later Peter's black button down flew through the gap and hit him in the face.

Bobbie's voice sounded again. "With the shifter out of the way the vampire, Lucien made his move."

"Hey, let me get my shirt on and finish my sandwich." Peter buttoned and tucked quickly, but it sounded like we were moving on.

The narration continued. "Lucien spun out of Thorne's grasp and swept out his leg, knocking him to the ground."

"Don't even think about it." I glared at Peter, who didn't really look like he was thinking about it, as he stuffed the last bite of sandwich into his already full mouth.

Bobbie continued, "Before Stacia could react, Lucien shot a broom handle through the double doors, preventing Xavier from offering assistance. Then, faster than humanly possible, grabbed a knife from the kitchen and held it to Crystal's throat. Stacia and Thorne, who had regained his feet, froze."

We all looked at each other. Penny walked over and grabbed a broom, that I would have sworn wasn't there before. She threaded it through the door handles, so they couldn't be opened. That got the rest of us moving. Kaitlyn came out from behind the table and stood by me, while Peter walked back to the kitchenette and grabbed the butter knife he used on his sandwich. He licked the peanut butter off, wiped it with the paper towel, then joined Kaitlyn and me.

"I don't think we've been formally introduced." He took her hand. "I'm Peter, and I'll be your abductor this evening." Kaitlyn giggled and allowed herself to be spun into his arms. He stood behind her and wrapped one arm loosely around her stomach and used the other to hold the butter knife in the vicinity of her neck. We waited for the next instruction.

Bobbie went on,

"'This will fail, DeFrost,' Thorne said.

'I think not, Hunter. In fact, this pretty little shifter may be exactly what I need to ensure my success,' the vampire replied. Lucien edged towards the door, dragging Crystal with him. Each time she struggled, he pressed the knife blade against her neck.

'Reach into your pocket, my dear, and get me the keys to the Jag,' Lucien instructed. 'Don't try to be clever, Sweet. I can smell that I've already pricked your delectable neck. It would take very little motivation to rip your throat out and gorge myself on your lifeblood, consequences be damned.' With a whimper, Crystal retrieved the keys and Lucien grasped them in the hand not holding the knife.

'I do understand that you are required to pursue me. I would expect nothing less. But if you value her life, and I know the puppy certainly does, you'll wait until I've left the property.' Lucien turned his face and buried his nose in Crystal's hair, inhaling deeply. 'You've no idea the level of control required to resist such a fragrant offering.' With that, he slipped out the door and into the night.

The secured double doors bowed as Xavier tried to force his way through. Stacia rushed to remove the broom, while Thorne followed the vampire, but he was too late. The Jaguar roared to life and sent gravel flying, as it burst from the drive onto the main road

Stacia and Xavier, seething with anger, joined him.

'My kit bag is still in the trunk,' Stacia said.

'We will need to resupply quickly.' Thorne turned back to the building. '*Were*, I trust you have a way to track your vehicle.'

Xavier gritted his teeth. 'Of course; Crystal's phone can be tracked as well. But I won't have to. She's my mate, I can sense her location, and I can sense what she's feeling. We need to move.'

'We will not proceed unprepared. Stacia, go pack a new bag. Include extra restraints and the collar.'

Thorne's unhurried manner sent Xavier's temper soaring. Stacia disappeared down the hall to retrieve the requested items. She didn't want to be in the way of the shifter's explosive temper. The species mated for many reasons, one being they balanced each other. A shifter deprived of its mate quickly succumbed to its volatile nature, a being that acts on impulse, to the peril of anyone who gets in its way," Bobbie finished narrating.

Chapter 8

Aaaand, Action!

Chase the Night

"Well, I guess we're out of here." Peter released Kaitlyn. "You heard her; I get to drive." He held his hand out for the keys, looking like a kid in a toy store with a fifty-dollar gift card.

"Nuh, uh. How can you drive and hold me captive at the same time?" My sister replied, straightening her coat. She took the knife from Peter and tossed it in the stainless-steel sink.

"Come on! It's like one of my top twenty dreams come true," Peter continued to plead as they headed toward the door.

Kaitlyn paused and turned to me. "I have no idea where we're going. This is where the pages she sent stopped. I'll see you at home, okay?"

"Sure," I said, still pondering the monumental weirdness of this new situation. I shook my head. Life with Penny so far, had not been dull. It made it difficult to imagine a future with normalcy. Buying a house, shopping for groceries, having kids. Would she even be happy with plain old Tripp? Then again, I didn't think her regular life was particularly action packed. This was the stuff we needed to be talking about, not just exploring our chemistry, as much as I enjoyed it.

Penny walked over and removed the broom, propping it against the wall. Gregorio emerged from the hall, buttoning the cuffs of his navy plaid flannel.

"What did I miss?" He looked around the room. "Where are Peter and Kaitlyn?"

"Bobbie narrated them away," Penny said.

Gregorio cocked his head to the side, listening. "That is strange. I can still hear her in my head." His brow furrowed, then he smiled. "And she does not much like it."

Bobbie's voice sounded from overhead. "Like Kaitlyn said, that's pretty much the end. Thorne sent Stacia to kit up, and Xavier out to start the van and begin tracking the Jag. Then they pile in and leave. I need to make a few changes in the next scene, so we probably won't be ready to read-in again until the weekend."

"Friday is better for me," I said. "But I can shuffle things if we need to do Saturday."

"We'll nail it down and let you know." Penny walked over to stand by me while Bobbie was speaking. She squeezed my hand. "We're going to take a few minutes before we get sent back." She guided me to the door.

Gregorio absently raised his hand in acknowledgment. He sat on the sofa, semi reclined, staring trance-like at the dark television screen. Though his eyes appeared unfocused, his expressions changed as if he were in conversation with someone. I supposed that meant he was talking to Kaitlyn. It was incredibly creepy.

"Hey, leave Kaitlyn alone," I said.

His eyes focused on me for a moment. "Your sister is a big girl, Trent. You tend to your own relationship."

I didn't have time to say anything else, or lay him out, before Penny dragged me out the door.

"It's fine," Penny said, after the door slammed behind us.

"What did he mean 'my' relationship? We're the only ones that have a relationship. He and Kaitlyn don't have a relationship." The thought of that guy with my sister made my blood boil as much as the thought of him moving in on Penny.

"You need to chill. We've already been over this. I didn't bring you out here to talk about Kaitlyn and Gregorio."

I took a deep breath. Kaitlyn didn't even like the guy; she wasn't going to be taken in by his charm. She was far too cynical.

"I wanted to talk about our timeline in person," Penny continued. "You know, we only have about three weeks before Cora moves in next door. Now, with the rewrites, it seems unlikely we'll be finished before then." She hesitated. "I'd like to make a plan to meet."

"Okay," I replied.

She hurried on. "Meeting in person won't be any different from this right here." She motioned between us.

"It would though. This is a fantasy. We can enjoy being together, hanging out, catching vampires," I said, trying to lighten the mood. "Out there, we have things, responsibilities, burdens taking up our time and energy. I feel like I'm a different person in here than I am out there."

She rubbed her hand down my arm. "What are you afraid of, Tripp?"

Wasn't that the question? If I shared all of my fears, I'd ruin this for good.

"What if we're too different out there? What if the chemistry or whatever isn't enough to overcome all the heavy life stuff? I mean, I don't have a lot of heavy life stuff, just the normal, my apartment, the store… I don't think I'm that different. What you see is pretty much what you get." For the most part, anyway. But she's exactly what I needed. I needed her life, her light, but it would be selfish of me to depend on her for that. I'd suck it right out of her.

"Tripp, it makes me think you do have a lot of heavy life stuff. Otherwise, it wouldn't bother you so much." She moved in closer and wrapped her arms around my middle, resting her ear over my heart. "Will you tell me? If this version of you I've gotten to know is the one without burdens, then he exists in real life, too. Let me help you carry them."

I laughed hollowly. "How about I open a vein, instead?"

She turned her head so she could look at me.

"I can't talk when you're looking at me like that," I said.

She buried her nose back in my chest. I loved the way she felt. I wanted to soak her up and keep her with me. I wrapped my arms around her tighter, trying to find the words to share something without giving away everything. "When I was active duty, I did three different tours in the desert. It was dicey sometimes. When I separated, there was a lot to unpack. I, uh, have a person that I talk to—check in every few months—through the VA. But that experience is always going to be with me. 'Out there', it's like a darkness, a shadow that's always there. It's part of my life and I don't feel like it's fair to force that on anyone else. And I feel… I'm afraid that if we meet for real, you won't like the real me, then I won't even be able to have you here like this. I'm being selfish. I'm being a selfish ass for not wanting to give that up." I opened my eyes. I didn't realize I'd squeezed them shut. Penny looked up at me again. Her face was damp, and tears clung to her eyelashes. "Please don't cry." I brushed the moisture from her cheeks. "I'm not worth it."

"Tripp," she breathed. "I've learned so much about you these last few months. The real you is chivalrous, kind, and funny. You're generous, open-minded, and have a mile-wide jealous streak. You're competitive, sharp, and protective. I love talking to you, spending time with you, figuring out this ridiculous legacy with you, *and* exploring our chemistry. You are worth it to me. You're worth my tears and my time. I can deal with your baggage. Is that all you were worried about?"

"Yeah, yeah it is." *Liar*. But at least she dropped the idea to meet in person, for now.

Chapter 9

Emerging Subplot

"That was wild!" Gregorio said, once we'd all acclimated to being back in my bookstore. "Bobbie, how did you do it? I changed from a wolf to human, I can talk to people using my mind, when do we go again? He braced his hands on the armrests, ready to launch himself out. I'd never seen him so excited. Gregorio was usually the epitome of calm and collected.

"All I did was write the story. What the legacy magic decided to do with it is beyond me." Bobbie smiled. "That was wicked cool, though. Sorry about the naked bit. I should have thought that through a little better."

"I don't think Kaitlyn minded too much." Peter rose from his chair to refill his coffee.

Gregorio looked abashed. "I should not have teased her."

"You didn't say anything rude, really. I'm sure she's fine," I said.

He tapped his head. "You did not hear all of it. I would never be rude, anyway. I responded to some of her thoughts she probably didn't want me to hear. I should have been a gentleman and ignored them."

Peter refreshed Gregorio's cup and handed it to him. He accepted it and relaxed back into his chair, coming down from the rush of his bizarre experience.

What did she say, er, think?" I asked.

"As a gentleman, I will not repeat it."

"It's not cool to dis and tell, Penny," Peter scolded.

Gregorio gave him an indiscernible 'guy' look, cocked up one eyebrow, and said, "She did *not* dis me."

Peter smiled wide and leaned back in his own chair. I looked between the two of them trying to pick out what I was missing from their subtleties to no avail. Fine, keep your bro-code secrets.

Bobbie made entries in her ever-present legacy notebook. A lot of crazy stuff happened this time, not even including Tripp's revelations, which I wasn't comfortable sharing with the group, so she was trying to get every bit written down before she forgot.

"I'll make sure it doesn't happen again, Gregorio. At least, I'll make sure you have privacy and clothes next time," Bobbie said as she scribbled. She finally put her pen down and closed her notebook. "I have a ton to do before Friday night. Peter, I don't think we'll need you and Kaitlyn next time. But to be honest, I'm kind of curious what will happen with your characters, if you're not in a scene."

"We know that there are only people in scenes we are currently playing out. The rest of the setting is deserted." I said, catching Peter and Gregorio up to speed.

Bobbie continued, "So what happens if you read into a scene you're not part of? Do you not go anywhere? Do you show up in the scene anyway? Do you go somewhere else?"

"Babe, are you saying you're going to science experiment with Kaitlyn and me?" Peter asked, sounding a little hurt.

"No, of course not. Well, sort of. But there has never been anything dangerous about the read-ins, even in all the grandmother letters. I'm confident there's no danger, other than the possibility of boredom." Bobbie stood and walked over to Peter's chair. She put her hand on his cheek and bent to kiss him. "I would never jeopardize your safety." After kissing him on both lips and temple she straightened. "Okay, we need to head out. I really do have a lot to do if this is going to be ready." Peter rose, rinsed his mug in the sink, and grabbed Bobbie's backpack.

"I must go too." Gregorio also rose. He respectfully pecked Bobbie and me on our cheeks and fist-bumped Peter. He seemed distracted, but he had much to absorb from tonight.

"Goodnight." I closed the door behind him and locked it. He responded in kind and headed up the sidewalk.

"Everything okay?" Bobbie asked as she and Peter moved to the rear exit where Peter parked.

"Yeah, everything's great. Tripp told me some things tonight that go a long way in explaining some of his behavior, his secrecy."

"Oh? Do you want to talk about it?"

I knew she would stay if I asked her to, but I also knew she was anxious to leave and get started on the new pages. Besides, I wanted to do some research on PTSD before I decided how to proceed with Tripp. Not 'if' I would proceed, because I'd decided by now that I was all in. I just needed to figure out the best way to convince Tripp I wanted this. It hurt my heart to know that he was a hero, but he only saw himself as a broken man.

"No, go on home and write some awesome scenes. I'll talk to you in a couple days. Hopefully, I'll have some 'bachelor' information to impart by then." I needed to get back to my research, much as I dreaded it. The search for the descendants of my many-greats grandmother, Elizabeth's potential suitors was daunting. After eliminating the first as a non-starter, the second led, unfathomably, to Gregorio. Nobody but Bobbie, and probably Peter, knew this, but Gregorio and I share Elizabeth and her husband, Danior as a common ancestor. Surprisingly, it was on the Irish side of his family, not the Romany. He probably had no idea his Romany genes came from both sides of his family. I'd undoubtedly tell him, someday, when the legacy dust finally settles.

Bachelor number three was a schoolteacher in Elizabeth's town of Westmeath. If he was supposed to have been her soul mate, and she'd waited to marry him instead of Danior, the gypsy love magic never would have turned into the legacy, or curse, I'm dealing with today.

By tracking down the descendants of Elizabeth's intended soul mate, my own granddaughter will have as much available information on our legacy as possible. The popular theory amongst the grandmothers is that when Elizabeth's descendent and the soul-mate's descendant finally get together, the magic will be fulfilled, and the legacy will finally end. It was just a theory, but it made me feel like I was doing something constructive to contribute to the completion of the family legacy. It hasn't been really bad for me, at least not like for a couple of my grandmothers. But ultimately, I think I would have preferred to meet Tripp the usual way.

I think we could have avoided some of his anxiety about meeting in person because under normal circumstances, that'd be the only option. I would also have been able to present myself as the real me instead of the weird girl with the gypsy curse. The whole 'by the way we're eventually going to get married' was a struggle to work around. As I finished shutting off lights and making my way to my apartment upstairs, I thought over the things Tripp finally shared with me.

His PTSD obviously didn't prevent him from running his business. But then again, I didn't really know much about that, other than 'sporting goods'. That made sense though; Tripp requested the next book be something active, but not necessarily basketball, like *Pom Squad* had been. I pictured camping and outdoors equipment. It fit with the fact he was a soldier; guys like that got into the whole wilderness survival stuff. Of course, he could just as easily own a pro golf shop.

I moved through my nighttime routine, trying to imagine the Tripp I knew in various sporting scenarios. I quickly discarded both track and power lifting; too bulky for one and not buff enough to be the other. 'Sexy archer' had merit. I'd been a Robin Hood fan since Costner played the role. 'Sexy mountain climber', I could imagine, too. I'd already seen his powerful calves at work on the basketball court.

Too wound up to rest, I slipped into bed and turned my thoughts to the research I'd be getting back to in the morning. Tedious and boring, it put me to sleep in no time, but Tripp was there waiting for me in my dreams.

****

I'd like to say that I respected Tripp's privacy when I sat down at my computer on Tuesday morning, but that would be an unfortunate falsehood. I was really quite ashamed of myself. For punishment, the universe prevented me from finding anything useful. My searches for Tripp + sporting goods, Tripp + sports store, and outdoors + Tripp, only gave me travel directions to every Academy, Bass Pro, and Cabela's in the area, and a few hits for road trips to scenic parks for good measure. It would have been helpful to know his last name and where he lived; East Coast was kind of a broad search area.

After a quick detour to search Costner + Robin Hood images, I closed the window and opened up my saved research tabs. We have O'Cionnaoith, schoolteacher, Westmeath, 1734, to 1766. It took me most of the morning to discover he had married a woman named Anne in 1756, fathered four sons and a daughter, then died of influenza in 1766, along with one son, sadly. His remaining sons were Peadar, Timothy, and Stíofán; one girl, Rachel.

I hated those big families; I never knew for sure which line to pursue. My own tree didn't have a ton of branches. Even so, the curse/legacy passed to the firstborn granddaughter. While researching bachelor number two, the shopkeeper, sometimes I would follow a son, sometimes a daughter. It's really amazing that it led me to Gregorio, and even more so that we shared a common ancestor. There was still a possibility that one of the shopkeeper's descendants will satisfy the legacy one day. For that reason, Gregorio's name will go in with my research to pass down to my granddaughter. Who knows, maybe my granddaughter and Gregorio's grandson will be the end of the legacy. Even between us, his relation is distant enough to not raise any eyebrows.

But my feelings for him were mostly platonic now, bordering on sisterly since my discovery. Besides, he wasn't my soul mate, Tripp was.

****

A slow morning at the shop had been conducive to getting my research started. I wrote Peadar at the top of a clear page, then shut my laptop. By being ready to go for tomorrow, I felt I'd accomplished something for today.

The bell tinkled over the door, and I looked up to see Gregorio coming through. He looked eager, and I could tell he was still excited no, giddy, from the reading last night, despite the nudity snafu.

"Good morning, Penelope." He looked at his watch and I noticed he carried a to-go sack from the deli around the corner. "Or should I say, good afternoon? I know Bobbie is busy, so I thought I'd bring you lunch."

Bobbie usually was busy, mostly with school but now with the added stress of writing and narrating the plot of my love life. I really couldn't ask for a better friend. My stomach growled as I shifted my research material to the side. "Please tell me there's a California club in there."

"Sorry, I will remember for next time. Your choices are muffuletta or ham and cheese on wheat."

"Either is fine; thank you so much. Let's eat in the nook." I grabbed two bottled waters from the mini fridge behind the counter and joined Gregorio. He handed me the ham and cheese with a bag of chips and traded me for a water. We settled in and ate in silence for a while, but I could tell he waited for a pre-planned opening.

"So," he began. "That was the wildest thing I've ever experienced."

I laughed. "Literally, right; because you were a wild animal?"

He brightened. "Yes, right." He chuckled, then mentally brought himself back on track to his original topic. "So, the telepathy with Kaitlyn. That was cool." His attempt at nonchalance failed completely.

"Mm hmm," I agreed while I chewed my sandwich. I smiled inwardly; I wasn't going to give him an inch. I would have had to been blind not to notice the sparks flying between Gregorio and Kaitlyn during the read-in. I may not be able to actually define it, but I certainly noticed it, and so did Tripp.

"So," he started again. I wonder if he even realized he repeated himself. "How well do you know Kaitlyn?"

"I don't really know her at all; you've probably spent more time talking to her than I have. Has she said anything about where she and Tripp live?"

"Our conversations weren't like that." He took a bite of his sandwich to avoid saying more.

Ah. "What exactly do you want to know about her?"

He swallowed his bite. "I don't know." He shrugged and took a drink of his water. "Do you think her hair is like that in real life?" Kaitlyn's blonde hair, heavy with waves, fell below her shoulder blades. In the *Pom Squad Mystery* it was the same color, sans bangs. Her cheerleader character bound it back into a bouncy ponytail, but I still remembered it being longish. *Chase the Night* was more modern than *Pom Squad*, so most likely, Kaitlyn's hair was true to life.

"Probably," I said. "When you're not a wolf, your hair looks the same as it always does."

He contemplated this for a moment. "Do you think she's a cranky person in general or just doesn't like me?"

I took a swallow of my own water to hide a smile while I formulated my answer. "I think that every time she sees you, you're harassing her brother." I quickly held up my hand to forestall his defense. "I know the harassment is mutual and mostly harmless, but I think she feels protective of Tripp and doesn't want to see anyone messing with him." I contemplated my own insight for a moment. Tripp was a solid guy physically. Why would petite Kaitlyn feel like she needed to defend him? Not only that, but her need to defend him practically made her immune to Gregorio's good looks, that is, until he turned up naked. She sure noticed then, but she wasn't happy about it.

"So, do you think she's seeing anyone in real life?" And there was the question he'd really been working himself up to ask.

"Tripp has never mentioned that she's dating anyone. I think they hang out a lot, and I can't imagine she'd have time to do that if she had a serious boyfriend, but I really don't know for sure-for sure."

"Well, I'm interested in everyone involved in this new venture; it's not a big deal. Have you talked to Bobbie? How is her writing coming along?" He drained the rest of his water and set the bottle aside.

"She had class yesterday and I haven't talked to her since Sunday. I need to text her and find out if we're meeting on Friday or Saturday. I know Tripp prefers Friday. Do you have a preference?"

"No, not particularly." He crumpled his sandwich wrapper and shot it into the trash. He collected the rest of the trash into the empty deli bag, and I rescued the water bottles for recycling. Gregorio had sort-of gotten the information he came looking for. Now he had work to do.

"I'll be next door for most of the afternoon, adding switch plates and swapping out some knobs. Let me know if you hear anything."

"I will. Thanks for lunch; it was perfect timing."

"You are quite welcome." He brushed a kiss on my cheek and left.

Chapter 10

Me Thinks

Kaitlyn was waiting on my parents' front porch when I got home from work Wednesday evening. She met me at my truck and grabbed, unnecessarily, my lunch bag and a small sack of groceries on the passenger side.

"I can get those," I grumbled.

"I know, but I'll take them up for you anyway." She turned and preceded me up the stairs to my apartment. She stood to the side while I unlocked the door.

"I'm not an invalid, you know." My ire rising.

"I'm not helping you because I think you're an invalid. Maybe I want something." She put away the lunch meat and cheese I'd purchased, then unloaded my lunch bag. She'd get to the point eventually. Hopefully sooner rather than later, I was exhausted.

While Kaitlyn hand-washed my breakfast and lunch dishes I grabbed a Coke from the fridge and downed two painkillers. I retrieved the meat and cheese she'd just put away and pulled a package of tortillas from a drawer. I made a quick wrap with the ingredients and tore off a bite, eating because I should, not because I felt hungry.

Kaitlyn put away my supplies and wiped the crumbs into her palm, depositing them in the sink. She opened the freezer and helped herself to a Fudgesicle before plunking down in the chair across the table from me.

"Are you ready to tell me what you want?" I took another bite, wishing I'd bothered to put my mustard on it.

"Can't I visit with my favorite brother?"

"No. I'm tired, Kate. Tell me what you want so I can go to bed."

She had the grace to look chastised. "Remind me again why we don't like Gregorio."

"I don't like him because he has a thing for Penny." Though honestly, I didn't really see any evidence of it during the read-in. I *did* see evidence of his interest in Kaitlyn, which gave me plenty of new reason not to like him.

Kaitlyn thought for a moment. "I think they're just friends."

"Now, maybe," I grumbled under my breath.

"No, really. From the telepathic connection we had," she blushed, "he seemed distrustful of you, but protective of Penny. Is there something that happened to make him feel that way?"

"No. I don't know. Maybe he knows that I've been less than forthcoming with Penny about what I am."

"*What you are?*" Kaitlyn snorted. "Whatever. It's not like you're some kind of Frankenstein's monster."

I ignored her. "She doesn't know where I live, or what, exactly I do, or even my last name."

"You guys talked last time though, right?"

"A little," I hedged.

"Did you tell her?"

"About the PTSD, yes."

"Seriously?!" She stood up and stomped to the kitchen.

I heard her pop the lid on my trash and toss the wrapper and stick.

"So basically, Gregorio's only guilty of being a stupid guy jerk like you," she said when she emerged from the kitchen.

"Yeah, but he's a smug, cocky bastard, too." She rolled her eyes so hard I could practically hear them. I rose to follow her to the door. "Why do you care? What's going on with you and him?"

"Nothing, I just needed to know why we didn't like him. But now I know you really don't have a good reason anymore to not like him, while he has plenty of good reason to not trust you."

"Again, why?" I demanded, ignoring her slight.

"Because I want to know about the guy who's spending so much time inside my head." She yanked open my door and stepped onto the landing. "And he's hot!" She slammed the door on my curse word.

I was done. I couldn't find my bed fast enough. At least the medicine would ensure a full night's rest.

Chapter 11

Permanent Vacation

"Hey, I didn't expect you today," I greeted Bobbie Thursday afternoon. I'd been pretty much manning the shop solo all week so Bobbie could work on the story when she wasn't in class.

"I wanted to go over some options with you before we read-in next. I think it's ready to go for tomorrow night, if you want to let Tripp and Gregorio know."

"What kind of options?"

"Not exactly options, but I wanted to talk through a couple different scenarios."

I perched on a stool behind the counter. Bobbie came around and joined me, opening the stepladder to use as a chair.

"The next scenes only really involve you, Tripp, and Gregorio."

I grimaced. It sounded more like I'd be playing referee without Peter and Kaitlyn there to run interference.

She continued, "Gregorio will still be able to talk telepathically with Kaitlyn. So, I'm wondering if Peter and Kaitlyn need to be present for this reading, since they won't have any action, or do you think if Kaitlyn reads in but not Peter, she'll be subject to the bad guy vampire character, like the margrave?"

I experienced some pretty harrowing scenes in *The Murderous Margrave*. Knowing it was completely fictional did nothing to temper the scariness in the moment. I wouldn't wish that on Tripp's sister and he probably wouldn't appreciate that kind of cavalier approach. "Is Peter not available or something?"

"He can do Friday this week but not Saturday or Sunday. His men's league is starting tournaments and it will take up most of his evenings for the next couple of weeks."

"Let's all read-in Friday and see what happens with Peter's and Kaitlyn's characters. If it turns out they need to be here for all read-ins, we'll have to get creative about scheduling," I said.

"Okay, thanks. I know you're trying to get done before Cora moves in."

"This is my deal. I wish it didn't mess up your life as much as it has. If it turns out Peter is required, we'll just not have Kaitlyn read-in when he isn't available. She might not like it, but the whole point is getting me together with her brother after all."

Bobbie visibly relaxed. I felt bad about putting all the additional pressure on her, but in my defense, some of these problems stemmed from her own foray into the world of paranormal fiction writing. I felt disloyal thinking like that. Bobbie had been amazing during this entire process; I couldn't imagine a better friend.

"I'm going to go home and make sure the story doesn't need any more edits. I'll see you tomorrow night."

"Okay, sweetie." I stood to give her a hug. "Make sure you get some rest." She waved off my suggestion and left. I returned to my stool and opened my laptop.

Bobbie worked so hard, I felt bad for slacking off in my research. Granted, I had until my death to get it done, but I wanted to be able to put it behind me, or box it up complete when Tripp and I finally started our lives together.

Peadar. The name stared at me from my otherwise blank notebook page. I sighed and pulled up the starred link to all things Westmeath. It didn't take long to discover Peadar had married a woman named Anne, like his mother; weird. They had two daughters, so I set him aside for the time being. My method had been to follow sons for as long as possible.

Timothy and Stíofán went into business together founding Oak Heart Distillery in a town near Westmeath. When I stumbled across a death notice for Timothy, my stomach turned over. I didn't even know these people but seeing the word *hanged* listed as cause of death, really threw me. It somehow made Timothy and his poor brother, Stíofán, seem real to me It also made me wonder what he'd done. How did you go from upstanding business owner to being a hanged criminal?

I lost myself and several hours down a rabbit hole of Irish history. I hadn't ever given any thought to what Elizabeth had lived through, nor what it meant to be a Catholic during that time; the people were treated so poorly. While looking for the distillery, I instead found information about a group called the Hearts of Oak, or Oak Boys, a protest group that didn't like the disparity of treatment between Catholics and Protestants by English Gentry.

They were forced to provide labor to build and maintain roads, then were expected to also pay tolls to use those roads, while the rich contributed nothing. They also protested extra fees paid to the Church of Ireland for marriages, baptisms, and funerals, even when said service wasn't even provided by it. If Timothy was trying to fight back against oppressors, he gave his life for it.

It made me sad. It also eliminated him from my list, since I'd not found any marriage information for him. I wondered what happened to Stíofán. I assumed the distillery was a front, or maybe a poorly disguised headquarters for their group. I couldn't believe Stíofán escaped unpunished.

I stood from my stool and stretched. I glanced at the clock, surprised to find I'd missed closing time by seven minutes. There were no customers, so I quickly rectified the situation. I cruised the bookshelves, straightening and re-shelving as needed. I turned out lights, collected my things, and headed upstairs, Stíofán weighing heavily on my mind.

I could set him aside and start working on Rebecca, but my gut told me Stíofán was my guy, at least for now. Once in my apartment, I deposited my laptop and notebook on the coffee table and put together an egg sandwich and fruit for dinner. I'd not found any further information on Stíofán; no marriage, no death, no arrest. Though, I didn't find any arrest records at all, so I probably wasn't looking in the right place or the information wasn't accessible with my limited skills.

My theory connecting Timothy and Stíofán to the Oak Boys was all speculation, but it fit and felt right. If Stíofán had been arrested, what would they have done with him? I munched my sandwich and typed 'Irish jail records, 1785'. I found a database that went all the way back to the 1600s. It listed the convicts' names, when and where they were tried, and their sentences. It also included each convict's birthplace.

I adjusted the parameters of my search and looked only for convicts from Westmeath. There were two for that time period, Timothy and Stíofán. Stíofán was convicted of lesser charges and shipped to the English colony in Barbados, as a slave. When his sentence ended, he was required to serve more time as an indentured servant to repay the state for his care and transport. Then he could be free or continue as a paid servant. His five-year sentence and additional three-year indenture moved my search 'across the pond' to Barbados. I'd welcome the change of venue if the circumstances weren't so depressing.

Chapter 12

Control Subject

"I'm not actually in any of the scenes." Kaitlyn pouted and tossed the new sheets onto my coffee table.

"Not physically, but supposedly you talk to the dog. Bobbie wants us all there in case things go sideways. She doesn't know if anything will happen with you and Peter or not." I passed her a Coke and settled into my recliner, grabbing the printed sheets from the table. "Ready?"

"Whatever," she replied.

Chase the Night.

Thorne and Stacia followed Xavier's *were* instinct several miles to a stretch of forest Stacia knew eventually ended at the sea.

"We walk from here," Xavier said. "This is part of the reserve. It's six thousand acres."

"Are you certain?" Thorne asked.

Xavier ignored him and got out of the van. He stood still. After a moment, he inhaled deeply, then focused his attention to the northwest. "Yes, I'm sure. Our connection is fading, but I can smell her, sense her."

"Where's the car then?" Thorne demanded.

Xavier didn't answer immediately. He gave Thorne a look of distain that would have cowed a lesser man. Stacia quickly interceded to defuse the tension. Brandishing the tablet, she showed Thorne a detailed map of the area. "If Xavier is picking up her scent from the northwest, they probably parked somewhere along this stretch here." She pointed to a spot about a mile ahead of their current location. "If they entered the woods here, they'll be traveling parallel to where we are now because this area," she used her fingers to enlarge the location she referred to. "Is rocky with steep inclines and jagged drop-offs. If he knows the area at all, he won't want to have to drag an unwilling hostage over that terrain." She reduced the page again and ran her finger in a line over the screen. "If we go this way we'll be on a path to intercept."

"Excellent work, Stacia." Thorne meted out praise sparingly, so it surprised Stacia to receive it. Xavier grunted. Thorne's approval or lack thereof meant nothing to him. He was anxious to get on with finding his mate.

"*Were*, grab the kit bag. We'll also need the tent and provisions," Thorne directed.

"I don't get paid for that," Xavier returned, surveying the woods for the best entry point.

Stacia shook off her confusion at Thorne's unexpected attention and made her way to the back of the van. It was actually her job to retrieve the items Thorne requested. Xavier, seeing Stacia hefting the heavy bags, walked over and relieved her of all but the kit bag.

"This is probably the best point of entry," Thorne called from several yards away. Xavier scowled, but joined him, taking over the point position. Stacia shouldered the kitbag and followed. She felt Thorne's eyes on her as he stepped in line behind her. She felt her cheeks heat at the surprising feelings Thorne's praise evoked.

"I'm kind of an ass, aren't I?" Thorne moved forward to relieve Penny of the vampire hunting kit. He swung it over his shoulder as he fell in step behind her.

Penny grinned at me. "You're an old guy, so I imagine you're pretty set in your ways."

Gregorio snorted a laugh, from up ahead—Jerk— and stopped so we could catch up. Wordlessly, he handed over the smaller of his burdens to me to carry. I grabbed it, but since it was a smaller backpack, I didn't protest when Penny took it from me, and slipped it onto her own back.

"Can you hear my sister?" I asked Gregorio.

"Sort of. I can't hear words, but I can sense her. It's very strange, like she occupies a corner of my brain."

"I hope it's a small corner," I mumbled under my breath.

Penny shoved into me with her shoulder, nearly knocking me off balance. Gregorio appeared oblivious to my comment, as he focused on the inside of his own head.

"And what is it you 'sense'?" I held a branch aside so Penny could pass.

Gregorio blinked at me and replied, "Extreme boredom." Yep, that sounded like Kaitlyn.

"If we keep heading in this direction, we should run into them. Maybe you'll be able to talk to her when we get closer," Penny stepped over a decaying stump.

"Yes. Keep heading northwest," Bobbie's voice said from the air. "Tripp, you and Penny should both have high tech compasses in your pockets, but it really won't matter. Keep walking, and when the story says you catch up to them, you do."

Penny groaned. "How far do we have to walk? I appreciate the full moon and all, but couldn't you write us a path or something?"

"You'll walk for an hour, then the canopy will block out the moonlight, and you'll have to make camp for the night," Bobbie said.

"Ugh! Walking and camping! I thought you were my friend."

"Not a camper?" I put my arm around her. "That might be a deal-breaker." I smiled so she'd know I was mostly kidding.

"I think, under the right circumstances, I'd like camping." She gave me a side eye, leaving me hopeful I'd be able to create the perfect circumstances.

Bobbie spoke again. "I know you're not much for wilderness exploring, Pen, but I'm afraid to try to rush it. If I try to write in shortcuts the magic will call me on it. We don't want another kidnapping incident."

"I know," Penny grumbled.

"No worries, Bobbie. I've got us covered," I said.

Gregorio was unusually quiet, not that I was complaining. He trudged forward through the dead leaves and undergrowth with an intense look on his face. Actually, he looked constipated.

"What's going on with Kaitlyn?" Penny asked.

I was embarrassed that I neglected to ask sooner. Nice brother.

"She's good, just bored and complaining about the hike," Bobbie said, confirming what Gregorio sensed earlier.

"What about Peter?" I asked.

"That's the weird part. The vampire isn't really Peter this time. He kind of looks like my Peter, but more what he'd look like in a police sketch artist's rendition. He doesn't talk, and because Kaitlyn is following without any trouble, he hasn't needed to approach her. I don't know what he'd do if she ran, but I asked her to please not try to find out."

"So you can't guarantee her safety?" I released Penny, ready to rush to my sister's aid.

"The Magic has never done anyone real world harm," Bobbie reassured me. I was not reassured.

Gregorio called from several yards ahead. "I have her!" He picked up speed, so I pulled Penny along behind me so we wouldn't lose him.

"The good news is, at this rate of speed you won't have to hike for the whole hour," Bobbie said.

"Gee, thanks," Penny panted.

I slowed; there wasn't any real need to keep up with Gregorio. We'd all have to stop and set up camp at the same place. Sharing a tent with Gregorio would be bad enough, I didn't want to risk Penny's affections by making her cranky with me beforehand. Continuing at a quick walk I reclaimed the backpack Penny carried despite her weak protest. I repositioned her hand in mine, so I held it rather than tugged on it.

"Thanks," she said. "I could have carried it, but I appreciate it."

"You're welcome. I used to enjoy backpacking. This is pretty light compared to what I've carried in the past."

"You probably lugged heavier bags when you were, what? Being a soldier, fighting? What term do you use?"

"Deployed is a simple enough answer." I shrugged. "Yeah, there was always stuff to cart around in the desert. Even when we weren't working, we had to carry our chem gear with us everywhere."

"I'm sorry. You said you don't like to talk about it."

"It's okay. Ask me anything, fair's fair. This is what we're supposed to be doing, getting to know each other." I felt like a cheat though.

"Let me think."

I had to keep in mind that, unlike past books, we weren't exactly alone this time. Bobbie could see and hear our every move. It prevented me from asking more personal questions, not to mention dog boy walking a couple of yards ahead. "I'll go first. Are you against all athletic activity, or is there something in particular you like to do? Other than cheerleading?" I added with a grin, referring to the last book we'd read together.

"Very funny. Would it be cliché to say I like long walks on the beach?"

"Do you?"

"It sounds like something I'd enjoy." She smiled. "Honestly though, I used to take riding lessons when I was younger, and even started competing a little until age fourteen or so and other interests pulled me away. But after our adventures in *Margrave*, it's been on my mind. Of course, I'm still too busy to give it serious thought. Have you ever ridden?"

I grimaced. "Hasn't everyone at one time or another?" I stalled. "I don't know that it's something I'd be interested in." Her shoulders fell. I couldn't explain that I didn't even know if I'd be able to ride.

"It's probably too tame for someone like you. It's okay." She perked up. "You already know hardcore camping and hiking aren't my thing, but I also don't really like basketball either. No one said we had to have the same interests."

"I've really been too busy running my business to

keep up with any extra-curriculars. I get my exercise at the gym like most of the population, lately. That's one of the reasons I've enjoyed these read-ins, I get to do things I enjoy without losing time in the real world." I realized my mistake when she wouldn't meet my eyes. "Of course, my number one reason has been getting to know you and your friends." I pulled her to a stop. I wrapped her in my arms and leaned in so I could speak directly in her ear, nuzzling her hair as I did. She smelled of eucalyptus and mint and I vaguely wondered if it came from her own shampoo or Stacia's. "Especially you. I have absolutely loved getting to know you." I spoke low in her ear. She turned her head so her lips would meet mine, and we took a moment to ourselves.

"Um," Bobbie spoke from overhead at the same time Gregorio crunched his way back to us. Stealthy, the man was not.

"The vampire's tying Kaitlyn to a tree so he can go hunt," Gregorio announced. "I think now would be a good time to go rescue her."

For once I totally agreed with the guy.

Bobbie, apparently, disagreed. "I know that's what your alpha-maleness wants to run off and do, but we have to stick with a plot. I promise you; Kaitlyn is fine."

I looked at Gregorio for confirmation. He shrugged. "She's pissed-off, but not hurt." He paused. "And her nose itches, but she can't reach it."

"See, she's fine. This is almost the end of the scene anyway. Your group makes camp for the night. There's no point in staying in the book if you're just going to be sleeping."

"Then why is the scene there at all? It would make more sense to skip ahead to the rescue." Granted, I'd tied

Kaitlyn to trees plenty when we were growing up, I knew she was fine. But endless tromping through the woods seemed like a boring chapter.

I could hear Bobbie give an impatient sigh. "In order for the plot to remain believable and still allow for the romantic component, Stacia and Thorne have to have intimate alone time."

Oops, I'd forgotten about that. "Well, what about him?" I jabbed a thumb at Gregorio.

"You and Penny pitch a tent," she sniggered, "and get some shuteye." I could imagine her making air quotes around the word shuteye. "Xavier is too worried about Crystal to sleep. Besides, someone needs to stay alert and ensure the vampire doesn't come snack on you."

Gregorio cut in. "Kaitlyn says to hurry the truck up and pitch the spam tent so the scene can end." He gave me a confused look.

"She's been trying to clean up her language by using word replacement ever since our niece repeated something she shouldn't have," I explained.

"Ah," Penny said. "At the basketball game she said something about a ship. It makes sense now."

"Here." Gregorio threw the tent bag at me, nailing me in the shoulder since I wasn't ready and still had an arm around Penny. Jerk. "You need help with that?"

"No, I can manage. Thanks for the offer." Not. "Penny can help me; it will be good practice for when we camp later. Under specific circumstances, of course." I winked at her.

She sighed and set her backpack down. "Anytime, Bobbie," she called up to the sky.

Chapter 13

If I Must

"I'm really concerned about the next scene," Bobbie said without preamble when she walked into the shop Saturday morning.

I had just cracked into a shipment of coffee mugs I'd decided to add to my inventory, since my customers seemed to come as much for my mediocre coffee as they did for books. There were six different quotes on them from classic books; I recognized four of the six. I figured the majority of my clientele would appreciate these more than mugs with Harry Potter quotes, which were my personal favorites. *Look at me, all making decisions good for my business.*

"What's this?" she asked before I could respond to her first statement. "Elmer Gantry was drunk. Call me Ishmael." She set her bag down and started really rifling through the box, reading off the rest of the mugs. "It was a dark and stormy night; The moment one learns English, complications set in.; It was love at first sight; These certainly have a range of appeal. I'm keeping this one, dock my pay." She re-wrapped a blue mug that read 'All this happened, more or less,' in bubble wrap and tucked it in her bag.

"So what's the problem with the scene?" I asked, bringing her back around to her original statement. Her keeping the mug didn't bother me, other than I'd now have to come up with something else to go with her birthday gift in a few weeks. I had finally honed my ability to procrastinate productively, hence the new inventory and the specialty coffee due to arrive any day.

"In the next scene, the vampire has to find a way to subdue Crystal during the day so he can sleep. I've planned for him to use chloroform so she can't yell for help or contact Xavier."

"Chloroform doesn't sound very vampirish."

"I know! That's the problem."

"Kaitlyn will not be on board with that." Neither would Tripp, and probably not Gregorio for that matter, if our lunch conversation the other day was any indication.

"That's the other problem. I don't want her to read-in this time since the vampire character might become violent if he's not Peter," Bobbie explained.

When we 'returned' from our last read-in, Peter was sitting just as we'd left him. "When are we supposed to start?" he'd asked, not even realizing he'd been left behind.

She continued, "Crystal and the vampire aren't part of the dialogue until you and Thorne show up for the rescue, so it shouldn't matter as far as the plot goes. I'll end the scene right after the rescue, or maybe right before… that's why I'm having so much trouble. I don't know whether to bother having Gregorio read-in this time either, since he won't need to talk to the real Kaitlyn."

I thought about what Bobbie said about the not-Peter vampire. "Let's have Gregorio go ahead and join us. I think it would be too weird having someone there who is essentially a stranger. Not to mention, we should probably make it a habit always to have a 3:2 ratio of real people to characters."

"Good point. If we have too many characters, they might try to force the original script. This is *not* the scene we want to risk that happening." She chewed on her bottom lip.

"All good?" I asked.

"Yeah, I think so. Do you need me to work a few hours this morning? I've been pretty absent this week. I'm sure you probably have stuff to catch up on. Now that we've sorted my plot problem, I can work from here as easily as home."

Because my fridge was empty and I was down to my last pair of clean jeans, I accepted her offer.

****

I put away a week's worth of groceries and ate a quick lunch. A check-in with Bobbie assured me all was well; she sent me back upstairs to take the rest of the day off. She claimed to need the paycheck, and suggested I use the time to continue my bachelor ancestry research. Darn her, she was right.

I left Stíofán in Barbados but had no idea how to track him from there. By my best estimation, his indenture lasted until at least 1780. Then he'd probably have to work longer to save money to leave.

I had difficulty finding information about specific people; instead, my search led me waist-deep into information about the African slave trade. It was infuriating and tragic. I learned that indentured servants, like Stíofán, were usually given land when their servitude ended. Being an island, Barbados didn't have much land to offer, so landowners would give land in

Virginia or the Carolina colonies. Because of this practice, landowners moved away from white servants and started solely using African slaves, who they never had to pay, release, or give land to. The thought process that allowed people to treat other human beings that way made me ill. I needed to get out of Barbados.

I decided to start looking for new land titles in Virginia and Carolina between 1779 and 1787. If I came up empty, I'd check Barbados again. But if this lead ended up being the right guy, he'd have to make it to America eventually, I assumed.

Good golly, this sucked. I sat back in my chair and arched into a stretch. I checked my phone, surprised to see I'd missed a text from Bobbie. She didn't want to bother me but had closed up shop and headed home. My stomach chose that moment to remind me it was indeed dinner time. Thankfully, that problem I could take care of. Stíofán would have to wait for a bit.

Chapter 14

The Calm Before

Kaitlyn was pouting again, but I wasn't surprised.

"Does Gregorio get to go?" She put her fists on her hips.

"Yes, but there's no danger for his character." I settled into my recliner. She could stand if she wanted to.

She snorted. "I've got moves; I could have handled the vampire."

"That doesn't matter. The plot doesn't say you handle the vampire. The plot says you succumb to the chloroform and pass out. Not going to happen."

"Why can't Peter be there again?"

"Basketball stuff. This isn't about you or Peter. It's about me and Penny. If we're both available, the story can move forward."

"Or you could meet her in person and spend all the time with her you want," she retorted, clearly not interested in listening to reason.

"Or maybe she lives a thousand miles away and decides I'm not worth the effort." The admission slipped out before I could stop it.

She came around the furniture and sat heavily on the couch. "You're ridiculous. She's totally into you. You guys will be able to work out any obstacle, but you can't start working on anything until you open up to each other."

"Which will happen soon, but not before tonight's read-in. You're welcome to hang out. Apparently, I'll only be 'gone' a split second."

"Fine. Then you can tell me all about it so I'm not behind the curve for the next one."

"Deal." I checked my watch and saw it was time. "Be back s…"

Chase the Night.

Xavier, once again in wolf form, bounded ahead. His connection to Crystal intensified with every step. Thorne and Stacia had no choice but to keep up or risk their opportunity to capture the vampire alive. Given free rein, the *were* would rip Lucian DeFrost to pieces for daring to harm Crystal.

Thorne did a better job of it, while Stacia was weighed down by a kit bag and a restless night. She knew she should focus on catching up and the danger ahead, but Thorne's confusing behavior continued to trouble her.

They finally stopped to rest the previous evening shortly after midnight. Xavier returned to his wolf form while Stacia sorted provisions and prepared a snack. Better to eat now, before sleeping in case they needed to get up and leave in a hurry. Thorne pitched the small hiking tent and unfurled a thin blanket and a mummy sleeping bag. Stacia watched him out of the corner of her eye, unsure how she felt about sharing such tight quarters with her boss. Though some of his recent behavior had been very unboss-like. The man was closed-off, condescending, and often arrogant. How could she even think about being attracted to someone like that?

She knew how. His confidence and skill in the field

were sexy as hell. She'd always had a weakness for men like that. Their difference in age didn't faze him; more proof he had the experience to back up his arrogance. Thorne approached and accepted the slow-release energy bar Stacia offered him. He ate it in three bites and chased it with a slug of water from his canteen. Stacia opened two more bars and left them for Xavier, hoping the chocolate chips wouldn't be a problem for his doggy tummy.

"We need to get some rest, or we won't be sharp enough to match wits with a vampire in the morning," Thorne said. "Xavier is concerned about what DeFrost will do to Crystal when he's forced to sleep come dawn."

"I'm worried, too. She isn't used to this kind of fieldwork. Her safety has always been a condition of the werewolves working with us. DeFrost knows she'll lead us right to him if she can."

"It concerns me, as well. We're not going to rest for long. Come." He guided Stacia to the tent with his hand on her back. "I'm bigger; let me get in first, and you follow."

Stacia stared skeptically at the tent. "This looks like it's only for one person."

"It is, but we need the body heat. Quit wasting time." Stacia scooted in feet first. It was impossible to avoid touching him, especially since his hands were everywhere, adjusting the bedding so it wouldn't bunch as she entered. Once in, her back and rear pressed against the side, distorting the tent's aerodynamic structure.

"It's not going to work like that. Stop being ridiculous." Thorne reached out and pulled her whole body snugly against his.

Stacia inhaled a shocked breath of Thorne-scented

air and stiffened.

"Get some rest," Thorne said gruffly and began rubbing her back.

Her senses were overwhelmed with the man and her reactions to him. Sleep seemed impossible. Other things, well, for the first time in Stacia's apprenticeship with Thorne, other things seemed entirely possible.

She must have been more tired than she thought because she woke to Xavier pawing at the tent and Thorne's body wrapped around her, spooning her into himself.

Distracted by the memory, Stacia ran smack into Thorne's back.

****

"Nice, Bobbie," I said. "If I'm going to have memories of spending the night with Penny, I'd like for it to have actually happened."

"Sorry, Tripp," Bobbie's voice said. "Penny and I may be BFFs, but any more than that would have been TMI for our relationship."

I turned to Penny, who seemed stunned from running into me. Though, she may also have been trying to reconcile her newly transplanted memories of our night together.

I leaned down and kissed her temple. "Don't worry, I still respect you."

She blinked at me, then smiled in understanding and playfully smacked me on the arm. I lifted the kit bag off her shoulder and transferred it to mine.

"What's next?" Penny asked when Gregorio trotted over to us. "Is he going to stay in wolf form for the entire scene?"

"No, I need him to be able to communicate with

you," Bobbie said. "There'll be a change of clothes in the bottom of the kit bag."

I set the bag down and pulled out a bundle along with a pair of hiking boots. I tossed them behind a clump of bushes not far from our path. The wolf gave me what I could only describe as a disdainful look before disappearing behind them.

"When Gregorio gets back, he'll be able to tell you what's happening with Crystal. We're almost at the point where the vampire is going to try to knock her out. Sunrise is about forty-five minutes away, and he needs to subdue her before he enters his hiding spot.

"Then what?" I asked.

"Then you rush in to rescue her while he's trying to transport her prone body."

Gregorio, fully clothed, emerged from the bushes. "That sounds dangerous; someone could get hurt." He frowned.

"Remember, right now, both the vampire and Crystal are characters. They can't really be hurt."

"Then what?" I asked, needing to make sure there weren't any big surprises in store.

"Well, the vampire disappears, and the hunters are back to square one."

"And then?" I prodded.

"Then I need to write some more," Bobbie snapped. "I need to make sure this scene works out okay before I go any further; otherwise, I spend all my time rewriting. Not to mention I have to turn your wholly unpleasant character into a feasible love interest for a girl twenty-five years your junior."

"And you're doing an amazing job!" Penny injected.

"Sorry." Bobbie let out a breath. "I'm just really

stressed about the scene."

"Hey, I think it's happening," Gregorio said. "This Crystal doesn't sound at all like Kaitlyn. She sounds, I don't know, more scripted."

I gave him a look. "Duh." Actually, I was glad for the confirmation that Kaitlyn hadn't somehow been drawn in this time.

Gregorio ignored me and continued. "He untied her earlier but has been towing her behind him with a rope. Now he's stopped. She's scared and struggling to get away. He's got her pressed up against some rocks, and he's trying to cover her face with a cloth."

Beside me, Penny listed to the right and stumbled. "I don't feel very good." She clutched her stomach. "I'm so dizzy."

"Pen!" I yelled. I barely caught her before she hit the ground.

Chapter 15

The One Where Things Go Sideways

I was going to puke, and not because I'd somehow teleported to an alternate location. Peter, or rather, Lucien DeFrost, was in my face, determined to suck on it. Not in the creepy vampire way, either.

"Stacia, I've never felt this way about a human before. My compulsion to taste your blood is overcome by my need to taste the rest of you," not-Peter, the vampire said.

"Eww. Stop." My word, his icy hands were everywhere.

"Damn it, I was afraid this would happen. I'm sorry, Penn. Are you okay?" Bobbie called down from the sky.

I self-assessed. "Yeah, I'm fine. Call off your fake boyfriend, would you?"

"Sorry!" She cleared her throat. "Lucien knew seducing Stacia would have to wait; dawn drew near. He smoothed his hand down her hair and stepped back. She affected him like no other, and he needed a moment before he could continue their trek."

"Gross, Bobbie. Really?"

She ignored me and continued narrating. "Lucien guided Stacia through the woods for about twenty more minutes until they came to a small stream."

"My love," Lucian Not-Peter said. "Climb on my

back. We must obscure your scent, otherwise you'll lead the wolf to our door." He chuckled at his own joke.

I rolled my eyes then climbed on his back. "Bobbie, I sure hope this is a means to an end." I tried not to freak out. Not that piggyback rides were intimate, per se, but I was generally not a touchy-feely girl. Okay, okay. I was very touchy-feely with Tripp, but this guy had a very not-Tripp feel and a not-Tripp smell. I didn't like it.

"I'm working on it. The original lines are literally appearing before me in bold print, so I'm having to make it up as I go along. I have to start over from scratch turning the plot around."

"Maybe not all the way. You've established the beginning of the relationship between Stacia and Thorne; that gives him a different motivation for following us. Also, now that I'm here, I'll follow your new lines. The vampire can still be in love with me, or whatever, but I don't reciprocate." My words tumbled as I bumped along on the vampire's back.

"But that puts us back to him having to do something with you while he sleeps because he can't trust you."

"He won't have to knock me out, though, because I can't communicate with Gregorio telepathically. He'll have to gag me. Um, or threaten me. I'm sure a threat will work just fine without having to resort to a gag."

"Crap! Hold on, I need to check in with them. Tripp's probably flipping out. Uhh…Lucien knew Stacia still resisted his charms. He would have to tie her up and gently gag her while he slept so she wouldn't escape."

"Hey!"

"Okay, hang in there. I'll try to end the scene quickly."

And then I was alone, clinging to the back of a stranger as he slogged upstream toward some jagged cliffs.

Chapter 16

You're Not the Girl I Thought You Were

"Bobbie! Bobbie!" I tried calling into the dawning sky again. Gregorio was no help, other than keeping the funhouse version of Bobbie occupied. Like the Billy character in *Pom Squad* hadn't looked exactly like Gregorio, Crystal looked like someone's description of Bobbie. Though, in this case, it was how Bobbie would probably like to describe herself. I remembered that Bobbie originally slated herself to play the Crystal character before things went haywire. This Bobbie was ten inches taller, at least four bra sizes bigger, and curvy. Very curvy. Her glasses were gone, and her hair a gorgeous mass of waves hanging midway down her back. She was, at the moment, trying to climb Gregorio like a tree. Gregorio appeared to be trying not to freak out. He kept removing the girl's hands and arms from his person, and verbally responding to whatever she was saying to him telepathically.

"Bobbie!"

"I'm here. Sorry. Is everything okay? Oh, my. Is that Crystal?"

"Is Penny all right?" That was my main concern. Her questions could be answered later.

"Oh, she's fine. The magic was not cool with the vampire's use of chloroform, so we've reverted back to the original plotline. Lucien is in love with Stacia."

Jealousy flared immediately. "What exactly does that mean?" I asked coolly.

"Are you jealous?" She laughed. "Don't worry, it just means he isn't interested in hurting her. She's already working on adjusting the plot."

"Bobbie, can you do something about this?" Gregorio asked. He finally resorted to wrapping his arms around Crystal in a tight hug that effectively restrained her roving arms. She now alternately kissed his chest and rubbed her cheek against his shirt front.

"Err, sorry about that. Umm. Crystal was mad at Xavier for not rescuing her quickly enough. She retreated to a stump beside their path, determined to give him the silent treatment."

Gregorio dropped his arms, and Crystal immediately stepped back, giving him a scathing look. She stomped off and planted herself on a chair-like stump I hadn't noticed before.

"Thank you. You know, Peter thinks you're beautiful, amazing, and sexy just the way you are. If I were not afraid he'd beat me up, I'd tell you the same," Gregorio said.

The guy was certainly smooth. I wanted to say something myself, but now I'd look like I was copying. "What happens now?" I asked instead. I could at least save Bobbie from having to respond to him; she was undoubtedly embarrassed.

"I need to get this scene ended so I can regroup. Gregorio, I need you back in wolf form, please. You can go behind the bush again for now. Since Crystal is with us, she'll be able to communicate between you and Thorne."

Gregorio nodded and headed off to the bush after confirming Crystal remained on her stump, pouting.

"Tripp, I think what needs to happen next is you guys follow the same trajectory for a while. Then Xavier picks up the scent when you come across the place Lucien tied Crystal up to go hunt. By then, it will be daylight, and I'll end the scene."

"It sounds like a pain to do all the rewriting."

"Oh, believe me, it will be. Just so you're aware, you could end my suffering by agreeing to meet with Penny in real life."

I put my hands up to fend off her words. "I have every faith in your skill as a writer. Besides, I want to know how the story ends."

"Whatever." She picked up the narration. "Xavier changed back into wolf form and led the group deeper into the forest. Soon, he began to pick up speed."

"He smells Stacia," Crystal informed me. She'd been following a few yards behind, dragging her feet and sighing, so we knew she was still grumpy with Gregorio.

"They followed the werewolf to a tree whose bark had been recently rubbed off in places," Bobbie continued.

"This is where I was tied up. Xavier says the vampire's scent is everywhere and he will be easy to track from here." Crystal gave the tree a confused look.

"You escaped and found us. Then the vampire kidnapped Penny, I mean, Stacia," I told her, hoping it would help.

Her confusion cleared, and she nodded her head. "Yes, I remember. I was very brave." She gave me a beautiful but somewhat vacant smile.

Bobbie continued, "Anxious to be reunited with

Stacia, Thorne kept pace with the werewolf. The sun crested the horizon; he knew their quarry would be stationary for the next eight hours or so, making it possible to avoid confrontation while rescuing Stacia. But Lucien's actions made this capture personal now. Thorne no longer cared if they captured the vampire alive. If he'd laid one parasitic finger on Stacia, he'd be wishing for death by the time Thorne finished with him."

Chapter 17

Barking Up the Wrong Tree

I was dragging Monday morning, after a late and long phone conversation with Tripp. He started off needing confirmation that I really was okay. Then we discussed mundane things about our lives. He told me about his family and his struggle to decide what he wanted to do with his life after separating from the Marines.

I told him about my grandparents and my own struggles with finding direction. It was almost two before we hung up. I hoped Mondays were slow days at Tripp's store, so he'd be able to chill and not have to deal with customers. I manned the bookstore. Mondays were one of Bobbie's regular days off due to her class schedule. She promised to drop in sometime midafternoon so we could talk about plot.

I had my laptop with me so I could continue my research, but my attempts so far proved fruitless. Apparently, Stíofán O'Cionnaoith left Barbados and fell off the face of the earth. Not really, I found no evidence of that. I found no trace of him whatsoever in North or South Carolina, within the timeframe I searched. I loathed the idea of starting back at the beginning with Stíofán's sister, so I set it all aside and decided to dust shelves until Bobbie arrived.

I wasn't really the creative type, but I at least knew Bobbie needed a place for the story to go without killing anybody off. At this point, it wasn't looking good for the vampire. Obviously, Tripp would rescue me, but the trick was to get Peter out of this unscathed as well. I think our little experiment with the cast failed, and we needed to make sure Peter, Kaitlyn, and Gregorio were all available from now on.

We had only a week before Cora took possession of the shop and apartment next door. With the rewrites Bobbie needed to accomplish, I didn't see any way we'd be done in time.

"Getting lots of research done, I see," Bobbie said, scaring the snot out of me.

"How'd you get in? I didn't hear the bell."

"You must have been pretty deep in thought." She scrutinized me more closely. "Or asleep. You look awful."

"Thanks so much. That's helpful."

"Just saying. We weren't up that late last night."

"No, but Tripp called." I went to the counter and stored my feather duster.

"Ah, I see. Any headway on that front?"

"Not on scheduling a meeting, no. We talked; it was nice. I can care for him and trust him even if I don't have all his life details yet. He's told me the important stuff."

"If you say so." She eyed me skeptically. "Let's talk plot. I have a study group in forty-five minutes, so we'll need to be quick." She remained standing while I settled on my stool.

"This is really your area. I don't have ideas, only opinions on other people's ideas."

"Well, we have a couple of options. I can try to force

it back onto the new storyline we were creating, with Crystal being the captive."

"That sounds like it would be easiest since you already had most of it planned out, in your head at least."

"The problem with that, is if we read-in and the magic refuses to let us make the swap, without a plan B, we'll be screwed," Bobbie said.

"You talk like the magic is a person."

"I almost feel like it is. A person who is supremely pissed at me for the chloroform mistake."

I rolled my eyes at her. "What's our other option, or plan B?"

"To leave it like it is and come up with a new ending."

"That doesn't really allow Tripp and I to spend any time together."

"You guys are going to have to suck it up and cut me some slack," Bobbie spat, then clamped her hand over her mouth. This uncharacteristic outburst told me she was under much more stress than I'd realized. "I'm so sorry, Penn. I know it's ultimately my fault we're even in this predicament." She looked close to tears.

I hopped off my stool and gave her a hug, then led her to the reading nook. "It's okay. I didn't mean for you to feel pressured. We aren't in any hurry." I ignored Cora's existence momentarily. "I know this is the last book before I meet Tripp in real life. I let my impatience override my common decency. I'm sorry."

"No, it's me. Peter's been so busy, I've hardly seen him. School's ramping up. I'm as anxious to finish up with this as you are. Not that it hasn't been an experience of a lifetime."

"Let's look at our options, maybe we can come up

with something so we don't have to rush. Where else besides here, and my apartment can we meet?"

"There are too many people around both my and Peter's apartments. What about Gregorio?" Bobbie suggested.

"I think it would be weird. We're friends now, but I don't feel comfortable asking him. Besides, he doesn't live close. What about Aunt Biddy?" She was the only other person on our end who knew about my family legacy.

"Um, that's a hard no. If we met at her place, she'd insist on participating. I don't want to have to plot around her shenanigans. We could meet at a park or something. No time passes while we're gone."

"I know, but I'd still feel vulnerable, exposed. I'd worry about random people there, too." I sighed. "Let's keep moving forward like we are. Surely, Cora doesn't spend every night at home."

Bobbie peered at me over the top of her glasses. "She's not exactly young. I bet she spends most nights at home."

"True. So do I, and I'm not exactly old. Shame on me for stereotyping. We'll figure it out." I patted her arm. "Do you think you'll have something by Friday night?"

"I should." She glanced at her watch. "I've got to go. If you have any ideas, give me a call."

"I will." I rose to follow her to the door. "And thank you, really. You're the best, best friend ever." I gave her one last hug.

"You, too." She returned my embrace.

The bell tinkled as she left, and I went back to look at the missing Stíofán mystery with fresh eyes.

****

Two days later, my research was at a standstill. Stíofán O'Cionnaoith had disappeared into thin air. At ten o'clock in the morning, I'd already downed four cups of coffee and run my fingers through my hair so many times, it resembled a lion's mane.

Thankfully, Wednesday mornings were slow, so I wasn't risking scaring off any customers. Murphy's Law engaged as I heard the bell over the shop door tinkle. I pulled my hair band off my wrist and quickly pulled my frayed curls into a chic messy bun.

"Good morning, Penelope."

"Cora, hi, please call me Penny. My mother and Gregorio are the only ones who call me Penelope. And I only let him get away with it because I love listening to him talk."

Cora giggled. "I know, he's a sweetie, isn't he? Are you two dating? I wondered."

I held up my hands to halt that thought "Oh, no, we're just good friends. I'm sort of seeing someone else."

"The tall boy?"

"No, that's Peter. He's with my friend Bobbie. I'm in a long-distance relationship." I stifled a laugh.

"Those are challenging; I wish you luck. What are you working on? I hope I'm not interrupting, Gregorio said I could drop-off a few boxes next door before the big move next week. I want us to be good neighbors, so I thought I'd pop in and say hello. I brought you some muffins I made this morning." She held up a brown paper sack I hadn't noticed.

I loved that Cora was willing and capable of carrying most of the conversation load. "I'm sure we'll get along just fine as neighbors, especially if you keep plying me with snacks." I took the bag and opened it. Mmm, blueberry."

"Are you researching your genealogy?" she asked as I chomped down on a muffin. "I don't mean to be nosy, but I caught a glimpse of a web page I recognize. I dabble myself. I can trace my ancestors back to seventeenth century French royalty on my mother's side. My father's side is Scottish and Irish; I'd only begun tracing it before I started packing to move."

I swallowed what had proven to be lemon-blueberry perfection. Maybe Cora could help me over this blockade in my research. "I'm not researching my own family, exactly. I read about an old boyfriend of my great, great, great, grandmother, and was curious to see where his family ended up after they parted ways."

Cora began leafing through my notes and looked up at me skeptically. "This is some heavy-duty research just to satisfy curiosity."

I gave her an innocent smile. "I'm like a dog with a bone when I get an idea in my head." I half-laughed. "I'm stuck now, though."

"Oh, what's the problem?"

"Well, I've traced this guy to Barbados where he was indentured. When his time ended, I think he may have been given land in the Carolinas. But I've looked through years of land titles and can't find him."

"Are you sure he left Barbados? Life was hard there; malaria rampant, he may have died."

"I couldn't find many records, but his name wasn't on any that I did come across."

"What was his name?"

"Stíofán O'Cionnaoith. He was Irish."

"Obviously." She chuckled. "That name is a mouthful. Are you sure he kept it?"

"What do you mean?"

"Many of the Irish, and other nationalities as well, changed their names to be less ethnically identifiable. Some names changed due to spelling variations or even because of dissimilar alphabets. Others wanted to disassociate themselves from their heritage when they came to the colonies to start a new life. Here, let me see." She dragged my laptop across the counter, turned it toward her and opened a new tab. "I can't remember the name of the site, exactly. Irish surnames changed over time," she mumbled as she typed. "No. No. No. Here, this one." She clicked the mouse and turned the screen so I could see it. When the page opened, she immediately scrolled down to a chart. "See? Brown used to be MacanBhreithium. Crazy, huh? You're looking for O'Cionnaoith." She scrolled some more. "There! You should search for Kenny or Kinney. It means 'fire sprung'. Pretty neat."

"Wow!" I quickly reclaimed possession of my laptop and bookmarked the site. "That's really cool!" This find infused me with new energy. When Cora left, I'd dive back in. Well, as soon as I polished off the second muffin.

Sensing my mood, Cora stepped back from the counter. "Well, I'll leave you to it then. I'm glad I could help. Oh, and here's my card." She pulled a slim card case out of her pocket and handed me one. "The office number isn't working yet, but you can reach me on my cell, I don't mind."

"Thanks for stopping by, Cora, and for the lead. And the muffins." I stopped short of telling her next time she should stay for coffee, because that would only highlight the fact I'd neglected to offer coffee this time. I felt bad for wanting her to leave so I could continue my search for Stíofán. I was a sucky neighbor.

"Good luck, hon. See you soon."

I'd already plugged the new name into my search site when the door tinkled closed behind her.

****

I closed my laptop with a satisfying click. Cora's tip almost immediately led to Stíofán Kinney. From there, my research took off like a grassfire. The Kinneys produced at least one boy child in every generation, and they all tended to stay in the vicinity of North Carolina, Virginia and Tennessee until the Civil War. Percival Kinney must have known something of his great, great grandfather's incarceration and wouldn't have wanted to be part of the Confederacy.

Once I found his name on the Union roster, I easily, well relatively easily, found the rest of his family living in northern Pennsylvania. I was only about one hundred and fifty years from present day. Record keeping should be a little more reliable from here on out. Kinney was my guy; I could feel it. Even after I found the descendant, I wouldn't know definitively if I had succeeded in finding the heir of Elizabeth's lost soul mate. In fact, I would never know because I'd be dead when my granddaughter inherited the legacy. I should be satisfied with a job well done; the fruits of my labors left for others' benefit. Too bad I wasn't that altruistic. I would probably sulk about it for a while or maybe low-key stalk the descendant; purely in the interest of keeping the research current, of course. Tripp really had no idea what he was getting into with me.

I was jumping the gun a bit, though. I hadn't actually found the guy yet. But soon, I was sure of it.

Chapter 18

ad hoc

The ice pack slammed into my stomach, barely missing my family jewels. "Watch it," I warned Kaitlyn. "What's your problem anyway?"

"I can't believe you still want to read-in tonight."

I shifted in my chair so I could position the ice pack on my hip joint. Kaitlyn was great about issuing care and concern in equal measure to her criticism of me. "I told you, I won't even feel this once we're in the story."

"And I still think you should rest. Don't make me call in the big guns."

"Do. Not. Call. Mom." There was no reason for her to ever find out about the altercation at the store tonight. Her brand of hovering was ten times worse than Kaitlyn's. I could have managed to keep it from Kaitlyn too, if she hadn't been here waiting for me when I finally limped home.

You had to be a special kind of stupid to rob a gun store owned by a former Marine. I pegged the guy before he even walked in the door. Larceny Pro Tip #1: Don't spend half an hour parked out front, getting toked-up on chemical courage, beforehand. It was almost seven P.M., closing time, when he finally approached the front door. Thankfully, the last customers were long gone, and Scott and I were closing up.

Pro Tip #2: Don't bring a knife to a gunfight. I had one hand poised over the panic button, and the other cradling my Glock 21. I'd sent Scott to the back of the store so he'd have the element of surprise, should I require assistance.

Pro Tip #3: When things start to go sideways, make sure your escape route is an exit and not a storage closet. The whole thing was practically a non-event. The guy, Chad was his name, cut and ran as soon as I drew my weapon. I would have emerged completely unscathed, had I not forgot myself in my rush to secure the closet door. I lost my balance, overcorrected, and landed square on my bad hip. Scott took care of the door while I picked myself up off the floor. I could already hear sirens in the distance.

We spent the next two and a half hours giving statements, closing the store, and putting a nice rifle on layaway for one of the detectives. All the hassle would be totally worth it if we could establish ourselves as the recreational gun source for the GMPD.

We weren't reading-in till ten that night, due to Peter's schedule. I was anxious to see Penny and put this day behind me. I hoped Bobbie figured out a way to put us back in a few scenes together. I picked-up the new pages I printed off at work. "Here, do you want to read ahead and make sure there's nothing too strenuous for me?"

She snatched them from my hand and skimmed the pages. "I told you I should have gone last time. You guys totally screwed everything up. At least I don't have to hang out with a vampire anymore."

Crap. That meant another night of not seeing Penny. I'd told Kaitlyn the truth. When I was Thorne, my injury ceased to exist. The same couldn't be said for my physical and mental fatigue. Being Thorne did nothing for either of those but being with Penny worked wonders on the latter.

"I think these pages are simply a means to an end. We hike through the woods, and Penny sits in a cave, while the vampire sleeps. The scene ends when we finally find the cave near sunset," Kaitlyn said.

"That sucks, but if it's what Bobbie needs to do to get the story on track, I'll deal." But I won't like it. I was too exhausted tonight to call her afterwards.

Kaitlyn handed the pages back to me and stomped to the kitchen. I heard the fridge, then the rattle of pills before she returned with a pop and ibuprofen for me.

"Thanks." I accepted her peace offering.

"I'm only going to see Gregorio. If for one second, you look like you're in pain I'm pulling the plug."

I didn't bother reminding her that wasn't how it worked. I wouldn't be in pain, so it was a non-issue. "Are you serious about Gregorio?"

She shrugged. "He's not as bad as I first thought. He's funny. And, like I said, he's hot."

I ground my teeth together. Not only would I not get to see Penny tonight, but it looked like I'd have to play chaperone for my sister and my least favorite person. If I canceled tonight, we'd just have to do the scene later, anyway. "Sit down, let's get this over with."

Chase the Night.

"He's lost the scent," Crystal said, as Xavier paced the riverbank. It was midday and Stacia had been missing for nearly twelve hours.

Thorne's agitation grew with each tick of the clock. "Keep searching. Obviously, DeFrost took to the water to mask his scent. They had to have exited somewhere; he was running out of time."

"The wind has blown away any trace that might have remained in the air. If we're going to start trekking blind, you're going to have to decide whether we go upstream or down," Crystal said.

"He would have headed into the mountains to look for a cave. He didn't have enough time to travel to the sea and his underwater lair," Thorne decided.

Xavier watched Crystal and Thorne's exchange. Decision made, he entered the stream and began wading against the current. The trio trekked on for miles, snaking their way up the mountain, as the stream led.

"Bobbie, I'm done," Thorne said. "Is there a way you can flash us to the end of the scene or something?"

"I can't flash you Tripp, but I can try to insert a page break," Bobbie replied.

"I knew it!" Kaitlyn said. "Is your hip hurting? Sit down."

My hip wasn't hurting, as I had known it wouldn't, but the total exhaustion of the day clung like a burr. I was in no mood, mentally or physically, to climb a mountain.

Gregorio exited the stream, either because we'd stopped or at Kaitlyn's telepathic request. He trotted over, then shook himself violently, drenching me before I had a chance to take cover. Kaitlyn, who'd managed to remain dry, knelt and pulled a towel out of her backpack. She beckoned the wolf to sit in front of her and she began vigorously rubbing his fur dry. Gregorio's eyes rolled back in his head in pure ecstasy.

"Someone tried to rob him this evening and…" she began to explain as she dried the wolf.

I cut her off with a sharp look.

"…and he's tired," she finished lamely.

Gregorio stared at me, as if trying to glean what he'd missed. He turned back to Kaitlyn, who opened her mouth then shut it again glancing at me.

"Kaitlyn," I warned.

She pasted a smile on her face. "I missed you," she said brightly, as she scratched behind Gregorio's ear.

His foot twitched and his tail thumped.

"You are just the cutest doggy!" She added her other hand and scritched her way around his neck until she practically hugged him. Gregorio panted and his tongue rolled out of his mouth. I wondered if Kaitlyn even realized her actions were akin to foreplay. She may not, but Gregorio sure did.

I snapped my fingers and his eyes blinked into focus.

Taking in my dark glare, he had the grace to look guilty before he scrambled back out of her reach.

"I think I figured out how to add a page break. It will cut out some of the setting description, and some internal dialogue, but you shouldn't notice," Bobbie said.

She was wrong. Gregorio lay down and covered his ears with his paws, whining. My vision blurred and my head started pounding with the worst headache I've ever had. Kaitlyn must have had a similar experience because she turned and vomited in the bushes behind us. I slammed my eyes closed and grabbed my head as my stomach turned over.

Suddenly, the pressure diminished, and my nausea passed. I opened my eyes a sliver. The rocks, trees, and stream hadn't really changed, but the sky was noticeably dimmer. It was a lot closer to sunset.

"I'm sorry guys. Was that too terrible? We're almost

to the end of the scene," Bobbie said.

I saw that Gregorio had crawled over to where Kaitlyn sat on the ground and rested his head in her lap. My head still ached, and I no longer had the energy to care about them.

"Don't ever do that again, Bobbie," I ground out.

"Please," Kaitlyn added. "It was like riding a roller coaster with a sinus infection and food poisoning."

"Eww. I'm sorry. Let me know when you're ready to continue."

"We're good," I said. "Let's just get this over with."

Kaitlyn rose unsteadily to her feet. Gregorio stood too, but remained in physical contact with Kaitlyn, offering silent support.

"Okay. Gregorio, you need to be back in the stream," Bobbie said.

He reluctantly approached the water. Shuddering, he waded in to await further instruction.

She picked up the narration. "Xavier suddenly became alert."

"He picked up the scent," Crystal translated unnecessarily.

Thorne knew they were close. Over the years, he'd developed a sixth sense about these things. He scanned his surroundings. Several crevices in the rock could lead into larger caves; he suspected trees and shadows disguised even more. Most were up high, making them more defensible for the vamp. Then he saw it, behind a clump of scraggly bushes, the hint of a fissure that would be shadowed most of the day. "There!" He pointed out the possibility to Crystal and Xavier.

The last sliver of sun, clung to the horizon, then winked out, leaving a thin line imprinted on Thorne's retinas. They were out of time. Not even the *were*, and its paranormal strength and speed could reach the cave, before DeFrost escaped with Stacia. He growled in frustration. Once she was safe, he would never let her out of his sight again.

"Shh," Crystal scolded. "You'll alert him to our presence." But her warning came too late. The vampire emerged, forcing Stacia in front of him.

"Hey, guys!" Penny called, waving.

I needed to touch her. After the hellish day I'd had, I needed to wrap my arms around her and feel her arms around me. Just the sight of her almost made me break down. "Can you come down?"

"I think we're supposed to disappear into the night, but I don't care." She turned to Peter. "Can you get us down? I rode up piggyback."

"Heck yeah," Peter replied. "Climb on."

I watched a little jealously as Penny positioned herself on Peter's back.

"I don't think I'll enjoy going down as much as going up, and I hated that."

Peter repositioned Penny's arms so they weren't crushing his Adam's apple. "Hang on, and probably close your eyes too."

Penny scrunched her eyes closed and Peter stepped off the edge of their outcropping. My heart skipped, as if I'd taken the fall myself, but Peter landed deftly on a boulder fifteen feet below. Penny let out an "Oof!" Two more similar jumps, and Peter landed in front of us.

"That was awesome, man, but if you ever put my…ah, put Penny in that kind of danger again, I'll strangle you," I shook Peter's hand, then proceeded to peel Penny, whose eyes were still shut, off his back.

"No need, bro. She's got it covered." He unwound her arms from his neck, where she'd left visible marks.

Penny's eyes popped open, and she quickly transferred her stranglehold to my neck. But I didn't mind; she could wrap me up like a kraken snack and I wouldn't care.

"Hours of boredom, ending with moments of sheer terror. I'll be glad when this book is over. I've missed you." Then her lips were on mine.

It felt so damn good I could almost ignore the guilt. It was my fault we were still doing this; my fault she'd been scared; my fault Kaitlyn had been sick; my fault Gregorio had been belly-rub blocked. Okay, I didn't feel any guilt about that, but it was my fault Kaitlyn was still wrapped up in this and not out looking for a normal relationship.

Like me, Penny might not be ready to set off on a happily-ever-after, but she was ready to be in a relationship with me, a real one. I could tell by the way she kissed me; our relationship had changed. She put more of herself into it; so did I, to an extent. Penny deserved all of me, I needed to convince myself I deserved her.

Chapter 19

When one door closes

Chase the Night and my meetings with Tripp were at a standstill. Bobbie was studying for finals in all her summer courses, and Peter's team made the playoffs, so he practiced more and traveled. Cora was taking possession of the space next door in two days.

On the other hand, my research on the O'Cionnaoith-Kinney family had exploded—in a good way. Despite the family's temporary move to the north during the Civil War, they managed to retain most of their property in North Carolina. They weren't some fancy-pants plantation owners. From what I could infer, they sold most of their land to fund investments; some lucrative, some less so.

Now in the twenty-first century, according to Google Maps, a Mr. Wendell Francis Kinney Jr. lived in a modest home in the suburb of Gypsy Falls, North Carolina. Don't think I didn't recognize the irony in this. He and his wife had at least one daughter and one son, maybe more. I was so excited to find a real, live son who could possibly carry the genetic code of the other half of my family legacy, I didn't bother to look any further. I couldn't wait to tell Bobbie, who was due to stop by any minute.

"So, what's the big news?" Bobbie asked, walking

in the door. "I only have a few minutes."

"I found him! I found the descendant!"

"Okay, that's great," she said, hesitantly. "How can you be so sure? I mean, I'm thrilled for you. But there are a lot of variables. I don't want you to get too excited about it, only to be let down later."

"Oh, I'm pretty sure," I said smugly. "The signs are all there." I handed her my notebook.

"Gypsy Falls. Are you serious?"

I grinned as she whipped out her cell phone and started typing. "This place is only about six hours away. We're going on a road trip this weekend."

"How do you have the time?"

"After Thursday, I'll only have one final left, but it's an easy one. We won't be able to read-in with Cora moving in, besides Peter has games every evening."

"What about the shop? You know, my livelihood."

"We'll leave after closing on Friday. You might consider closing an hour or two early, and Peter can open Saturday morning. It will be fine, so long as we're back by three."

"I don't know. What will we do? Not introduce ourselves?" I said.

"No, we'll drive by and check out the house, maybe park and walk by."

"Like creepers?" Though I did like the idea.

"Aren't you curious? You could meet the grandfather of your future granddaughter's husband."

It took me a second to sort out that statement. "We're not meeting anyone. Just looking."

"Right, that's what I meant. I have to say, Penn, I hope the whole name thing dies out before your granddaughter's husband is born. I'd hate to see the daughter of my future goddaughter saddled with Wendell Francis V." She shuddered.

"Fine. We'll take a road trip. But you have to stop sorting out my future relations. You're making me have to think too hard. Besides, I haven't even asked you to be the godmother of my future daughter yet."

"Yippee!" Bobbie clasped her hands together. "I'll make all the arrangements and book a hotel. And of course, you'll ask me to be your daughter's godmother, silly. I've gotta run, I'll text you later." She paused and became serious for a moment. "And thank you. I really, really needed a break from everything."

"You're welcome, always." I gave her a quick hug before she escaped out the door.

I found myself looking forward to the trip as well. It would certainly keep my mind off not being able to do a read-in or see Tripp. I ended up doing a little more research but came up with nothing but dead ends for Wendell the third. I even scanned the death records for the area with trepidation, but thankfully came up empty there as well. Maybe Bobbie and I could do some low-key stalking and figure out a way to strike up a conversation with Wendell II. I envisioned scenarios where an older gentleman was trimming his hedges or collecting his mail, so we could just walk up and talk to him. We could even knock on the door and say we were doing a survey for a college class. No, we are trying to find our dog. I'd have to find a random dog picture to print and take with us. We could even use our road trip and say Fido, no, Max escaped when we stopped for gas. Tentative plans in place, I started making lists for Peter for Saturday morning.

****

111

Bobbie finally managed to drag me out of the shop around two on Friday for our trip, under assurances that Peter would call me immediately if he needed anything. Gregorio also promised to stop in Saturday morning to see if Peter needed anything.

Cora was mostly moved in. She planned a grand opening for her shop the following weekend. Since we weren't reading-in this Saturday, I scheduled a housewarming for her after closing. Friday morning, I ducked out of the bookstore while it was slow to hand-deliver invitations to the neighboring shop owners. It felt good to be part of this community.

"How much farther?" I asked Bobbie, who insisted on driving so I could be the navigator.

"GPS says about an hour. Our exit is in 30 minutes."

I pulled up my own map app, so I could look for a place to eat in Granite Mount. "Should be some neat old buildings. Granite Mount hosts the United States' oldest active granite quarry." Finished with the ancestry stuff, I'd spent the past two days researching Gypsy Falls and the surrounding area. I wanted to know all about the place the heirs to Elizabeth's magic had lived for the past two hundred years. I supposed someday it might also become the home of my own descendants.

"And Gypsy Falls used to be called Gypsum Falls. The gypsum mines closed in the late 1800s, and the town's population dwindled. Then, in the early 1900s, a large influx of Romani immigrants moved in and petitioned for a name change."

"I thought the term Gypsy was considered derogatory," Bobbie said.

"I suppose it is unless you choose to use it on yourself. They really capitalized on their culture to make the area unique. There's been a popular medieval fair there every summer since 1975 with a heavy Roma flavor."

"That's really interesting, and weirdly coincidental, all things considered," Bobbie said, keeping her eyes on the road.

"It is, and it isn't," I continued. "The Roma contingent that made their home in Gypsy Falls originated in Romania. My family legacy originated with Irish travelers."

"That's the name of the bed and breakfast we're staying at; Travelers Inn," Bobbie said.

I enlarged my screen so I could check out local businesses. "Bogacha Bakery, Vagabond Threads, Caravan Security Systems and Storage," I listed off. "Definitely a community that embraces a theme. That's pretty cool."

We rode in silence for a while longer, then Bobbie took the exit for Granite Mount. "Did you find a place to eat yet?" she asked me.

"Meh. For all Gypsy Falls' local flavor, Granite Mount just has the normal stuff you find anywhere. But I'm starved, so Chillburgs is fine. And it's on our route through town."

"That's disappointing; we'll have to get our fill of old-world traditional fare tomorrow—after we build up our appetite stalking, that is." She winked at me.

We drove through Granite Mount while I alternately watched out the window and followed our dot on my map app. "It should be up here on the right. Do you see the pepper sign yet?"

"No, trying to watch traffic here. It's after rush hour. I'm surprised the roads are still so busy," Bobbie grumbled.

"It's in five hundred feet, right after the Mc—Stop! Stop the car!" I grabbed Bobbie's arm.

"Unsafe, Penn! Stop it; you're going to make us wreck!"

I wrenched my body around in my seat, afraid if I took my eyes off the building, it would disappear. "Sorry, but you've got to pull over and turn around."

"What is it?" she asked, picking up on my panic as she pulled into the fast-food parking lot.

"I only caught a quick glimpse. Can you please get on the road going back toward the highway? Stay in the right lane; we'll need to pull off pretty quick. I need to see if I saw what I think I saw." My hands were sweaty, and my pulse thundered in my ears as I forced myself to sit correctly in this in my seat.

Bobbie pulled out of the side parking lot onto the adjacent street. We waited for the light to allow us to return to the main road. She was quiet as she took a left turn and maneuvered into the right lane. I think I freaked her out.

Unblinking, I kept my eyes glued to the passing storefronts. Pawn shop, Taco Casa, check cashing place, Tripp's Trigger Supply and Range. "Stop!"

"Chill. I see it." Bobbie turned on her blinker and eased into the parking lot.

Chapter 20

What the What?

I regretted answering my sister's call. "No, Kater, we're not reading-in this weekend. Something about Peter's schedule and a new neighbor." Cora, actually, Penny had said when she called earlier to give me the bad news. I vaguely remembered meeting her in the last book, older woman, garish makeup, dressed like a teenager in 1955. I wondered what she looked like in real life. Maybe one day I'd find out.

I ignored Kaitlyn's litany of complaints and considered putting her on speakerphone so I could move on to the other tasks I needed to finish before closing. "Listen," I cut her off. "Why don't you come up and hang out anyway. I'll be done in about thirty minutes... No, the AC is on the fritz, so I sent him home. No need for us both to be miserable," I responded when she asked if Scott was there. "I do *not* need help closing the store. Last week was an anomaly. There's never been any trouble before."

I watched as an SUV pulled into the parking lot. It was one of those little ones that I had trouble taking seriously. My typical customers drove beefy trucks or four-wheel-drive vehicles, equipped for hauling camping gear in and dead animals out. Not to stereotype, but I'd bet money it was some chick looking for a frou-

frou purse gun or a gift card for her dad or boyfriend. I hoped for the latter; a quick, easy sale, then I could work on getting out of here. That is, if she or he would hurry and make up their mind about coming inside. The occupants of the vehicle were making no moves to get out. In thirteen minutes, the doors would be locked, regardless.

Finally, a door opened. "Kaitlyn, I gotta go, customers. I'll see you in a bit. Order pizza or Chinese or something." I disconnected the call as two women approached this entrance. No, not just two women. Penny and Bobbie. Penny was smiling nervously. Bobbie wore a frown but looked determined. How would they have found me? Think about that later; they were coming through the door.

"Tripp?" Penny stopped inside the door.

Bobbie crowded in behind her, allowing the door to shut. I could tell the minute she registered oppressive heat and humidity inside my store.

"Penny, what are you doing here?" I started to come out from behind the counter. Shit. I'd worn cargo shorts today in deference to the heat. I wasn't ready to spring the bionic man on her.

Before Penny could answer, Bobbie cut in. "What are we doing here?" Sarcasm dripped from her words like the sweat down my back. "This is your sporting goods store?" She used air quotes around 'sporting goods'.

I knew Bobbie could be fierce, but I sensed she was ready to remove my hide on Penny's behalf.

Penny placed her hand on Bobbie's arm. "It's not a lie, Bobbie. Hunting is a sport," she murmured, glancing around at the displays, then said to me, "It's because you were a Marine, your interest in guns?"

I shrugged, not taking my eyes off her. "It's what I know. I don't really hunt myself, though." I hoped to soften her impression if she was some kind of animal activist. There was still so much I didn't know about her. This encounter, strangely, felt less real than seeing her in the book. Maybe *I* felt less real. The real me rode horses, played basketball, and chased vampires through the woods. This me didn't do any of those things, not anymore. This me didn't hunt, animals or people. The former, due to lack of desire. The latter, thanks to a strategically placed roadside bomb in Iraq.

"I used to a little, with my dad. When I was a kid." She didn't say anything else. It was nice to see I didn't have the market cornered on awkward silences.

"Do you live here? And, oh my gosh, why is it so freaking hot in here?" Bobbie demanded.

"Here? In the shop? No. The AC guy couldn't get me in until tomorrow morning."

Penny took a few tentative steps closer while Bobbie fumed at me. Once again, I forgot myself and almost stepped around the counter to meet her.

"Do. You. Live. In Granite Mount?" Bobbie asked more specifically.

Still watching Penny, I answered, "No, I live in Gypsy Falls."

Penny's brows shot up, and she turned to Bobbie, then back to me. "What's your name?"

Confused, I said softly, "Penn, it's Tripp." Man, how I wanted to hold her.

"No, your whole name, your last name."

Crud. I didn't share my name with anyone. My mom didn't even use it when I was in trouble. Why did Penny want to know? "Kinney. My last name is Kinney."

"Is your first name Wendell?"

She shocked me speechless. I recalled the fairy tale my mom used to read, Rumpelstiltskin, and wanted to scream, 'a witch has told you; a witch has told you!'; an extreme reaction, true, but *nobody* knew that name. When I turned eighteen, I legally added 'Tripp' as my first name and dropped the III. My dad was a little put out about it, but he didn't go by 'Wendell' either. Everyone called him 'Junior'.

"Well, is it?" Bobbie snapped.

"It was," I conceded. "But how do you know that?"

Penny stepped closer still. "I've been researching parts of my family legacy…" she began when the shop door opened.

"We're closed," I said immediately.

A guy in a ball cap looked at me, then at the girls.

"They're finishing up a private consultation. We open at nine tomorrow. Please come by, and I'll help you with whatever you need; ten percent discount," I added. I just needed to get the guy to leave. He was familiar, but not a regular. I walked over and put my hand on his shoulder. "I'm Tripp, the owner. Sorry about that, but I appreciate you stopping by. I'll throw in a free hour of range time for your inconvenience."

"No problem, man. Thanks," ballcap guy said. He shook my hand as he left. I waved him out, turned the closed sign, and locked the door. I turned to find both girls staring at me with confusion and pity. Damn.

"Is that why you wouldn't meet me?" Penny stared at my prosthetic leg.

"I didn't want to spring it on you. I wanted you to know me."

"But I do know you. At least I thought I did. If you think your leg makes one bit of difference to me, then you obviously don't know me very well. Did you honestly think it would matter?" She didn't give me a chance to respond. "You know, people," she cast a hard glance at Bobbie. "Suggested you were hiding something from me. But I said, 'Oh no, I trust Tripp. He just wants us to get to know each other.' I trusted you, but you couldn't trust me with this." She shook now as she spoke.

"Penny, let me explain." I glanced at Bobbie for support, but only encountered her sad, disappointed look.

"No," Penny said. "I'm going to need some time. Even relationships built on gypsy magic need to have trust. We need to decide if we want to start over from scratch building that."

"Penn, please." But she turned away from me. I'd never seen her angry, and it bothered me that it was directed at me the first time I witnessed it.

"Bobbie, we need to go." She stopped at the door and turned the lock. Fresh air buffeted me, cutting the humidity as she walked out.

Bobbie followed, stopping to put a friendly hand on my shoulder. "She just needs to work through it; give her some time. I'll talk to her."

I rolled my eyes. I got the impression Bobbie was not my biggest fan at the moment.

"Men make stupid mistakes based on unfounded assumptions about women. But I am always on the side of true love." She followed Penny, and again, a mild breeze cooled my skin. I watched them pull into traffic and disappear. I relocked the door and limped back around the counter. My cell still lay there from my conversation with Kaitlyn. It felt like hours ago. I no longer felt like seeing anyone tonight. I planned to be too busy wallowing.

Chapter 21

The truth will set you free from the road paved with good intentions

"Are you okay?" Bobbie asked.

"Not really. I don't know. Can we just drive through Mickey D's instead of going to Chillburgs? I need some distance."

"A rib sandwich makes a poor substitute for baby backs with barbecue sauce. Let's head to Gypsy Falls and see if we can grab something there."

Granite Mount wasn't a major city, like Raleigh or Charlotte, but there was still a noticeable difference between it and Gypsy Falls. The suburb had managed to retain its small-town feel, probably thanks to the red brick buildings that made up the private college located near the center of town. Well-manicured green spaces and parks invited residents to socialize outdoors. And when the sun finally set, signs indicated there would be a free movie on the library lawn.

"Do you want to check-in first or drive by the Kinney house?" Bobbie asked.

"You said we have till nine-thirty to check in, so let's go see the house before it gets dark."

A few minutes later, we turned onto a street with old three-story homes set in narrow, but deep lots. Homeowners didn't seem terribly concerned with keeping the historical integrity of the homes, and many had additions, garages, and carports. A few places boasted impressive gardens in the front, while others used the lawn for overflow parking. Children played under a sprinkler in a yard littered with toys. Overall, it was unexpectedly unpretentious. That relaxed me somewhat.

"It's this one here," Bobbie slowed the vehicle to a crawl. The tall, white house looked faded compared to the two-story one-car garage that had been squeezed into the space on the right. A narrow, paved path separated it from the main house, but there wasn't even space for trash cans on the left side between the wall and the neighbor's fence. The garage stood about ten feet closer to the street than the house, and a wooden stairway led to the apartment above. The driveway had been widened to accommodate two vehicles. I could see a dark-colored pickup in the open garage and a blue minivan in the drive. Parked behind the van sat a newer, mint green Volkswagen bug.

"Park down the street a little way. We'll do a walk-by," I instructed Bobbie.

As we walked casually back toward the Kinney house, we passed an older gentleman trimming his hedges. I recalled my previous plans to arrange a conversation with Wendell Jr. What a turn this day had taken. No way was I up for conversation now. Besides, I'd forgotten my lost dog pictures in the car.

We reached the edge of the Kinney yard when a blonde woman came out of the house's front door. She went to the garage and shut the automatic door, then climbed about five steps up to the apartment and sat down, seemingly to wait.

"Kaitlyn?" I said, apparently louder than a whisper.

The woman's head snapped up. "Penny? Bobbie?" Utter confusion. "How are you here?" She rose and came toward us. We made up the difference and met her in the middle of the driveway. She greeted us each with a hug.

"Hey," I said nervously. "We were just in the neighborhood."

"Actually, it's a really long story," Bobbie said, saving me from a lie.

"And I bet it has everything to do with Tripp canceling our plans for this evening. Is he meeting you here? I was going to wait and interrogate him when he got home, but now I get to rub it in his face that I met you first."

"About that... I kind of already did."

"Oh?"

"Yeah. Oh," Bobbie said.

"And was there a problem?" Kaitlyn asked. I thought I could hear a hint of accusation in her voice, but I couldn't be sure.

"It shocked all involved, and Penny's a little put out with your brother right now," Bobbie said.

"Why?" Yep, definitely some defensiveness there.

"Because he didn't trust me and because he made assumptions about how I'd feel if I knew all about him."

Kaitlyn's shoulders relaxed. "Yeah, I'm not surprised. I've been nagging him to tell you for weeks. It wasn't fair to you. You needed to know what you were getting into."

Now it was my turn to get defensive. "I have no problem whatsoever with Tripp's leg. He's a hero, and I will be proud to be with him," I said hotly.

Kaitlyn laughed and reached out to squeeze my

hand. "I meant, you needed to be aware you were getting an insecure, stubborn, and misguided male specimen, that's all. I know perfectly well what Tripp is and what he is not. But all the love in the world won't disabuse him of the idea that he's broken." She turned to Bobbie. "Now, I really want to hear this long story."

The front door opened again, and an older blonde woman poked her head out. "Kaitlyn, dinner. Oh, I didn't know you had company."

"Mom, this is Penny and Bobbie from, ah, book club."

She ventured further out onto the porch, drying her hands on a dishtowel. "I didn't know you were in a book club, Katie."

"It's online," Bobbie said. Good save.

"Why don't you girls come in for dinner? I'm Diane."

"Oh, no, we couldn't," I started to back away.

Bobbie's stomach took that moment to growl loudly.

"Come on." Kaitlyn snagged us each with an arm and towed us to the porch. "They'd be glad to stay, Mom."

"So, what are you reading in your book club?" Tripp's mom asked us as we sat down to dinner.

"Fantasy fiction," Bobbie said.

"Paranormal romance," Kaitlyn responded at the same time.

"Ah, it's a little bit of both," I said. "The story has a lot going on."

I could tell by the sudden look on Kaitlyn's face she just had an idea, and that I wasn't going to like it.

"Penny and Bobbie were in the club before me. The

book we are reading now is part of a series, but I haven't had a chance to read the other books yet. Why don't you fill me in now and save me the trouble?"

I gave her a tight smile. "What an excellent idea, Kaitlyn. But I'm sure your mom and dad would be bored to tears."

"Nonsense! I'm always interested in what other people are reading. It keeps me from getting in a rut with my own interests; broadens my horizons. And Junior will tune us out anyway." Diane cut in.

We were introduced to Junior, or Wendell II, when we arrived, and he joined us at the table.

"I can't say she's wrong." Tripp's dad chuckled. "I've got one ear tuned to the game in the other room. Don't mind me."

Diane gave us a look that said 'see' and settled-in to hear about our fabricated book club.

Kaitlyn filled everyone's bowls with stew, and we passed around biscuits while I wordlessly conferred with Bobbie. She seemed resigned, but confident, so I let her start.

"Well, the series is about a girl who discovers that her great, great, great grandmother bought a love spell from a gypsy but ended up not using it."

"What a funny coincidence that we live in Gypsy Falls!" Diane said.

"That's what attracted me to the club in the first place, but Bobbie and Penny aren't from here, they came to visit me," Kaitlyn said

"Why didn't you tell me? I would have made a dessert."

"We're a day early," I blurted. "We hadn't planned on imposing."

"It's no imposition at all, hon. I just thought I'd raised my daughter to be a better hostess. I didn't know you were coming tomorrow, either." She frowned at her daughter.

"We were going to meet in town, not come by the house."

This seemed to somewhat mollify Diane, so I picked up the story's narrative.

"Anyway, since the grandmother didn't use the love spell, it passed from grandmother to granddaughter all the way to present day."

"What does the spell do?" she asked.

"It causes the granddaughter to get sucked into whatever book she's reading. While there, she meets the man who is her true love. He's actually a real person somewhere, but he doesn't know he's a character in a book."

Bobbie took over. "So the first book is about the heroine discovering and learning about her family legacy through a bunch of letters from past grandmothers. Then she ends up in an old book called *The Murderous Margrave*. She meets the guy, and at the very end, gets him to realize he's a real person and not a character."

I didn't know if we were explaining this very well. Kaitlyn knew enough to fill in most of the blanks. Hopefully, Diane would be satisfied with this abridged version, but not interested enough to want to read it herself.

"Now, the second book had a competing love interest, didn't it? I came in at the very end of that story," Kaitlyn explained to her mom, then smiled at me.

I narrowed my eyes at her. She was a sneaky one. "Sort of. He was in the first book a little too. They found out that when the girl, Jenny, went into a book, people who were nearby got pulled in, too. So the neighbor she'd been dating ended up in the story a couple times."

Bobbie continued, "Which of course added conflict to Jenny's relationship with the hero, her true love. But they worked it out. Now the only thing left is for the couple to find each other in real life."

"Does that happen in the third book?" Diane asked.

"Yes," I said. "Turned out the hero was hiding what he thought was a shameful secret."

Kaitlyn continued before I could work up a new head of steam over her brother's idiocy. "This is the book that's the paranormal romance. It has a vampire, a werewolf, and vampire hunters."

"Oh, that sounds like an exciting series! Kaitlyn, you'll have to get me the author's name; I'd like to read it." Diane smiled.

Crud! I was afraid of this. Bobbie, thankfully, was quick on her feet. "Unfortunately, the series is exclusive to our book club. We serve as beta readers for a small publisher. We won't know for at least another year if it will ever go to print. That's why Kaitlyn hasn't been able to go back and read the ones she's missed. It's a you-snooze-you-lose situation." Poor Diane looked crestfallen. "But Kaitlyn will for sure let you know if the series gets published." I hoped to ease the bad news.

She recovered quickly and made a topic change. "Where are you visiting from?"

"We're from Upper Orrington in South Carolina."

"Oh, that's far."

"About five hours, but we're staying at a bed and breakfast here in town," Bobbie said.

"That'd be the Travelers Inn. Nice little place. The

owner claims to be a descendant of the Gypsies who originally settled in Gypsy Falls. But Junior's lived here all his life and knows Connie's family didn't move here until the fifth grade. Isn't that right?"

Wendell grunted in assent, proving he had indeed given us half his ear.

"Has Kaitlyn introduced you to her brother, Tripp?"

Okay, so this was the direction the conversation was going. I didn't quite know how to answer that.

Bobbie saved me again. "Kaitlyn mentioned his store, so when we drove through Granite Mount, we stopped in to get further directions to her house. We met briefly."

"He's single you know, such a shame. He's quite handsome." She gave Bobbie and me penetrating looks over the rim of her water glass while feigning nonchalance.

"Bobbie's practically engaged," I said quickly.

Diane's eyes darted to Bobbie's left hand, which was currently reaching for the biscuit basket.

"Practically," Bobbie mumbled.

Diane shifted her laser focus to me. Gulp. "What did you think of my boy?"

"Mom, geez, you're embarrassing her. And you're foiling all my plans to set them up." Kaitlyn winked at me.

"Sure, I wouldn't mind a date with your brother," I agreed. Or marriage. Or kids. Or finally ending my family's curse.

"Fabulous! How about—"

"Mom, don't worry, I'll handle everything."

"But you know how Tripp can be."

"The last thing he needs is his mom meddling in his

love life. I can finesse him a little more subtly. And if that doesn't work, I'll steamroll him."

"OK, but he might be seeing someone already."

"What? Who?" I cut in. Nothing nosy and weird about that, but Diane answered me anyway.

"I'm not sure, he's never brought anyone around. And honestly, he's probably not treating her right because he's home every evening. But he seemed to be in better spirits, and I thought that might be why."

I relaxed and my cheeks warmed, happy to think I was probably the cause of Tripp's better mood. Wait a minute! I was still mad at him.

"Don't worry, Mom. I'll get him sorted out."

"Thank you for dinner; it was better than what I expected this evening." Bobbie glanced at me to see if I caught her slight at my fast-food recommendation.

"We need to head out so Bobbie can find the bed and breakfast before it gets too dark," I added, rising from the table.

"Thank you, girls, for such an entertaining evening. I'll count on seeing you again sometime soon." Diane gave Bobbie and me each a mom hug.

"Yes, yes, come back anytime," Kaitlyn's dad rose and faded back into the living room.

"I'll walk you out," Kaitlyn followed us to the door. "It looks like Tripp is home," she said as we crossed the yard. A newer pickup sat in the driveway. "He's probably upstairs sulking. I'll go harass him after you leave. Shall I relay a message?"

I thought for a moment. "No, I don't think so. I suppose it's too much to ask to keep our visit a secret."

"Even if I tried, you know Mom would spill the beans. We never did talk about how you ended up here."

"There was no way to work it into our book club tale," Bobbie said. "I'm even surprised your mom bought that."

"It just proves what a talented storyteller you are," Kaitlyn said. "So, what's the deal?"

"In the grandmothers' letters they theorized that the magic would be satisfied when one of Elizabeth's descendants hooked up with the descendant of the guy who should have been her true love," Bobbie said.

"I've spent the past four months tracing the families of the three possibilities Elizabeth mentioned in her letter," I added.

Kaitlyn's eyes went wide. "Is Tripp the guy?"

"It seems like a very strong possibility," Bobbie affirmed.

She squealed. "That is so freaking cool!"

Chapter 22

Unexpected Gift Horse

We pulled into the Traveler's Inn as we lost the last of the daylight.

"Look! We're right next door to Gypsy Falls Riding Stables." I pointed.

"Surprise," Bobbie deadpanned. "That was actually supposed to be your big surprise for this trip. I thought you deserved a reward for finishing all the research, 'cause I know how you hate it. Also, I felt bad for not including any horseback riding in *Chase the Night*."

I leaned over the emergency brake and gave her a heartfelt, if awkward hug. "This is a great surprise. You're too good to me."

"Good, I'm glad you like it. We have a trail ride scheduled for tomorrow at nine."

"You're going with me?"

"Against my better judgment. I'm considering it penance for not telling you I wrote the book."

"It'll be fun, you'll see."

An eccentric older woman checked us in. She dropped her fake accent after we mentioned we were acquainted with the Kinney family. She showed us to the bedroom with two twin beds and pointed out the communal bathroom down the hall, then left us to our own devices.

"I didn't realize the two-bed room didn't have an attached bath. Sorry," Bobbie said.

"I'm just thankful we're the only ones here this weekend. I think this is meant to be a children's room, for when families stay." I pointed out the selection of colorful books on the small shelf. "It's perfect for us. We can stay up late and talk without having to share a bed."

"So, you want to talk?" Bobbie asked. "Are you ready to sort out your feelings about seeing Tripp and Kaitlyn?"

"And their parents. My first feeling was 'thank goodness. Tripp looks more like his mom than his dad!'"

We both laughed at this. Tripp's dad could more easily be described as cuddly rather than handsome. The hair remaining on his balding head was dark brown. Tripp and Kaitlyn were both blonde like their mom.

Diane was healthy mom-shaped, and still had cheekbones most models would kill for. Tripp's chiseled facial features definitely came from his mom's side, but his blue eyes came from dad. While Tripp's were dark and intense much of the time, his dad's eyes were warm and wise. And despite favoring his mom, I suspected one day, Tripp's eyes would crinkle at the corners when he smiled just like Junior's.

"They seem like a really nice family. I know it seemed like his mom was only concerned with his love life, but I got the impression that she really worried about his emotional well-being," Bobbie said.

"Well, if the fact that he didn't want to tell me about his amputation is any indication, she's probably got a reason to be concerned." I leaned back against the headboard.

"Is he getting any outside help?"

"He did mention once that he saw someone, I assumed it was for his PTSD, but I guess it probably covers everything." My phone beeped with an incoming text from Tripp.

—*Can we talk?*—

—*I need time.*—

—*How long are you in town?*—

—*We're leaving tomorrow.*—

—*Can I see you?*—

—*I need more time than that. I'll contact you when I'm ready.*—

—*I'm sorry. I'd like to try to explain.*—

—*I will contact you when I'm ready. Promise.*—

—*Message received. Goodnight, Penny.*—

"Tripp?" Bobbie asked since I completely ignored her in the middle of our conversation.

"Yeah. I told him I'd let him know when I was ready to talk."

"Don't leave him hanging for long."

"Why not?"

"Well, in his mind, it may reinforce his idea that you can't accept his disability."

"Me being mad at him has nothing to do with his leg. Not really. It's more like an adjacent concern. Or a byproduct problem. Ugh. I'm mad because he lied by omission and because he thought I was a superficial person without giving me a chance. After all our conversations I thought he knew me better than that."

"Well, maybe he felt like he couldn't trust you completely because you were holding back information."

I opened my mouth to deny this, but Bobbie cut me off.

"I know you held back your location because he did. I get it, tit for tat. But you didn't tell him about your research. You didn't explain about passing down information."

"What was I supposed to say? By the way, I'm researching potential dates for our granddaughter and guess what, Gregorio's my long-lost cousin several times removed. He would have run for the hills."

"Now aren't you making assumptions about how he'd react?" Bobbie asked.

I grabbed my toiletries pouch out of my bag. "I'm going to brush my teeth. It's getting late, and it's been a heck of a day." With that I escaped into the hallway.

After I returned from the bathroom, we stuck to mundane topics; school, Peter, the book shop. Bobbie already made her point about Tripp, there was no need to say anything else about it.

****

Our hostess served breakfast between six and eight in the morning. Bobbie and I slid into our seats at seven forty-five. Connie told us our thin pancakes were traditional Romani blini. These were the sweet version to be filled like crepes with the whip cream and fruit she also provided. She said she alternates weekends serving these and the savory version to be stuffed with meat, cheese, and egg.

"Like breakfast burritos?" I asked.

She frowned at me and huffed back to the kitchen.

Bobbie soothed their hostess's feelings by making a big deal over the Romani tea she served with our meal. I felt bad for being so prickly. Hopefully, a sunny trail ride would improve my disposition.

After breakfast we loaded our bags into the SUV and

drove to the neighboring parking lot.

"I'll go check us in." Bobbie headed to the building marked office.

I wandered over to the corral and leaned on the fence. From there I could see another rider tacking up in the stable as a wrangler led a horse into the corral. The beautiful paint was already saddled and ready to go. Strangely, the saddle had a back and armrests. I also noticed, instead of stirrups the footrests were longer and covered the toe. There were also buckles, I presume for keeping the foot in place. Now I was curious who needed all those bells and whistles to ride. I hope they weren't prepping the paint for Bobbie. She may not like to ride, but I was confident she didn't need armrests.

Out of the darkness of the barn emerged a woman in jeans, riding boots, and a purple scrub top. Struggling to follow, another woman carried a boy, who I guessed to be seven or eight, but he could have been six or eleven for all I knew about kids. One thing was obvious, he wasn't having it. The woman, mom, I assumed, held him around the waist. His legs hung motionless, but his upper body twisted in her arms like a fish out of water. His arms crossed tightly while he twisted and thrashed his torso against her. He didn't yell but grunted in frustration.

The wrangler stepped forward and none-to-gently removed the boy from his mother's arms before she dropped him. The boy stilled at the unexpected change of confinement. The wrangler walked a little way away and plopped the boy on a fence rail, supporting the furious boy's upper body with his hand. The boy didn't have use of his legs, and his arm movement seemed somewhat restricted as well.

The woman in the scrub top talked to the mom, who

nervously watched her son.

I nervously watched him, too. The wrangler was reading the poor kid the riot act, pointing to the horse and to the mom. The boy sat rigidly with a mutinous expression on his face. The kid was handicapped for goodness' sake. He should probably go easier on him.

The man picked the boy up again. The boy allowed it but held himself rigidly.

"I can't do it!" the boy said loud enough for me to hear.

The mom wiped her eyes as she and the other woman looked on.

As the wrangler carried him toward the horse, the boy began to look less angry, but more fearful. Fear tinged with longing. Instead of putting the boy in the saddle as I'd expected, the wrangler brought the boy to the front of the horse, talking calmly to him the whole time.

Unlike mom, the man was able to support the boy with one arm. He used his other hand to gently unbend the boy's arm and guide his hand in petting the horse on the forehead.

Once the boy had mastered the motion, the man dug two apple slices out of his pocket. He fed one to the horse, then helped the boy hold his arm and hand correctly to feed the horse the second slice.

For the horse's part, I'd never seen an animal behave so gently. I would swear its lips never even grazed the boy's hand when it took the fruit.

The two went back to talking and petting the horse. The boy became agitated and started shaking his head. "No. I can't do it. I'm too dumb. I'll fall and everyone will say I'm stupid."

This seemed an irrational connection to make. No one equated falling off a horse with intelligence, but then again, I wasn't eight-ish and handicapped.

The man continued speaking softly to the boy, as you would to an agitated horse, ironically. He eventually did gently settle the boy into the saddle, helping him grip the armrest and adjusting his feet in the footholds.

At this point, the woman in scrubs joined them, and the two adults flanked the horse and boy as they made their way slowly around the corral.

Moments later, the mom joined me at the fence, still teary-eyed and watching nervously.

"Parenting sucks," she said.

"Pardon?" I replied.

"I feel like a monster, forcing him to do this, but I know it's good for him and he'll end up enjoying it."

I wasn't sure. The boy's face reddened with embarrassment and the adults had to keep reminding him to hold on to the armrests.

"Hmm mm," I agreed.

"Finn has been like this since birth, but in the past year, he started to become hyper-aware of how others perceive him." She wrung her hands together. "He's such a smart and funny kid, but now he's embarrassed by his infirmity. He won't try new things for fear of failure. His doctor wants to get him up on crutches eventually, but Finn is being stubborn. He recommended hippotherapy to help strengthen core muscles and build balance and hopefully his confidence, too."

"That sounds like good advice. Horseback riding is great exercise." I didn't really know what else to say. I was far out of my comfort zone with this conversation.

Echoing my thoughts, she said, "It breaks my heart

to see him so upset, but it hurts even more to see him withdraw. I can't let him spend his whole childhood ensconced in his comfort zone."

The scrubs lady was a physical therapist. She showed him how to relax his hips and move with the horse's gate. By the time the horse and company were on their fourth loop around the corral, Finn was smiling. He had even grown comfortable enough to raise one hand to quickly wave at his mom.

Bobbie came out of the office and beckoned me to follow her to the barn.

"It was nice meeting you." I waved to Finn's mom. "Good luck with everything."

"Have fun on your ride. I didn't mean to unload on a perfect stranger but thank you for listening."

I hurried to catch up with Bobbie. "We'll have to be quick if we want to get back in time to relieve Peter." I peeked at my watch.

"He called while I was checking us in. His game tonight cancelled, so we only need to be back to set up for Cora's party. I told him we'd be there about five o'clock. He was cool with it."

"Unexpected, but awesome. Peter's a keeper."

"Don't I know it."

The trail ride was beautiful, and well-marked so we were approved to go without a guide once we demonstrated proficiency on our mounts. I rode a pretty mare named Taffy and Bobbie rode an older black horse named Sprint, who thankfully didn't actually do much of that anymore. The extra time boon we'd received allowed us to take the longer trail which led by the waterfalls the town was named for. They were pretty, but unimpressive size wise. I guess I expected something like Niagara smack in the middle of town, not a minor canoe challenge hidden in the middle of the woods. It was totally picnic-worthy though. I'd have to bring Tripp out sometime.

Tripp. I wonder how he'd compare himself to Finn. So many things about a relationship made sense now. In the books, he had both legs again. No wonder he wasn't in any hurry to stop book hopping. How many things did he have to relearn? Horseback riding would surely be easier for him than for Finn. I wondered if he had ever tried.

I realized Tripp hiding from me wasn't really about me at all. He was probably a lot like Finn, except that he used to be able to do things.

His fear overrode even the trust he had in me. I tried to wrap my brain around someone like Tripp being afraid. Whatever name you wanted to put on it; embarrassment, uncertainty, lack of confidence; it all boiled down to fear. We could work around this, but I still wanted him to take a timeout to think about it. I would need the time, too. This was more than just PTSD. I needed to look up info on families of amputees.

****

"Do you want to stop?" Bobbie asked as we drove back through Granite Mount.

I waited to answer until we were almost in front of Tripp's store. Bobbie slowed.

"No. Keep going," I finally answered. I saw his truck parked at the end of the lot but couldn't see inside the windows. He was probably frothing at the bit because I wouldn't let him explain himself. Now that I'd had time to thinks about it, I understood more than he probably realized. Thank you, Finn and Finn's mom.

Chapter 23

'Bout Time

Bobbie and I arrived back at the shop a little after four o'clock.

"Where did all these cars come from? I'm going to have to park down the street," Bobbie said as we cruised by.

"Bobbie, all those people are inside. Stop the car and let me out. I think Peter is getting overrun. Crap! I knew we shouldn't have left on a Saturday."

Bobbie let me out, then continued to find a parking spot. I opened the shop door, already shifting into customer service mode, only to be confronted by flowers and balloons.

"Where is Bobbie?" Aunt Biddy, Peter's grandmother, demanded.

"Parking the car." The familiar faces surrounding me weren't customers: Peter's parents and brother, Bobbie's parents, Gregorio, and a few other close friends of the couple. "She'll be here in a minute. What's going on?"

"Grand gesture, Penn," Peter explained in a way that explained nothing.

"Here she comes," Biddy fussed from her lookout spot.

"Stand over here." Peter moved me to the side.

Everyone else moved, too creating a path from the door to Peter, where he bent down on one knee. Oh. I got it.

Bobbie came through the door like me, looking prepared to handle hordes of crazed bibliophiles. She stopped short when her eyes landed on Peter.

"Ah-hem. Bobbie Benton, would you do me the honor of agreeing to become my Mrs.?"

Bobbie put her hands on her hips and attempted to suppress a grin. "Pretty ballsy to do this in front of all these people, Celansky."

"Babe, we've been talking about it for two years. I was pretty confident. And look, with everyone here, they won't have to ask anymore when I'm going to man up."

"Ah, so you just saved me the pleasure of getting to tell everyone my good news?"

Peter hesitated, suddenly unsure of his plan. Luckily, Bobbie didn't leave him twisting for too long.

"Peter Celansky, I would be honored to wear your ring and own you." She closed the distance between them.

Peter slid the dainty square-cut diamond on her finger, then stood and scooped her into a hug that literally swept her off her feet.

Everyone, of course, cheered and clapped with a few 'about times' thrown in.

"I hope it's OK I commandeered your shop, Penn. I couldn't think of a more romantic place than a bookstore for my girl," Peter said after he set Bobbie down.

"Of course, it's okay. I'm excited to be a witness." Excited for Bobbie but a little more bummed about my own situation.

"You're the best." He pulled me into a bear hug. "I figured you could use the balloons for Cora's thing later."

"Oh, right. There's not much for me to do. Selma, from the bakery, is bringing the snacks when she comes. I just need to add ice to the cooler of pop."

"I can help." Gregorio appeared at my side.

"Great. Come on."

He followed me up to my apartment to retrieve the ice bags, then back down to the shop storage area where I'd stored the cooler. "How did your trip go? Peter mentioned you went on a girls' weekend." Gregorio helped me dump the ice in.

That was an understatement. Since Gregorio didn't know about my research, this would be a much longer answer than he probably anticipated.

"It was… enlightening. How much did Peter tell you?"

"Nothing really. We were blowing up balloons." He flashed his amazing grin.

"Well, it's a bit of a long story. But, since the shop is essentially closed, I probably have a few minutes." I sat down on top of the ice chest and Gregorio, seeing me settle in, grabbed a chair and straddled it backward.

"Tell me about it."

I decided to start at the climax and work back. "We met Tripp and Kaitlyn in real life!"

His eyes grew large. "Why would Peter not share that?"

"He might not know. It wasn't exactly the purpose of our visit to the area." I went on to tell him more about the letters and my research, including the part about us being loosely related.

He looked at me contemplatively. "It is indeed a very small world."

I continued to tell him about our final clues, our quest to find Wendell Kinney II, and how we ran into Tripp, who happened to be Wendell Kinney III.

"How did he respond? Did you discover why he kept himself from you?" Gregorio's voice took on a suspicious edge.

"Yes."

He raised his eyebrows in question.

This was Tripp's secret but keeping it from Gregorio might make it seem a bigger deal than it needed to be. The point I wanted to get across to Tripp was that his prosthetic was not a big deal. Sharing might also help Gregorio understand Tripp and soften his harsh opinion.

"I may have mentioned that Tripp is a former marine."

Gregorio nodded.

"He's also an amputee, from being injured overseas. When he's in the books with me, he has his leg back."

"I can now understand why he wanted to do a third book, but it wasn't right of him to not tell you."

"I know, and he knows. We need to work through some things, and he needs to work through stuff on his own. There are a bunch of emotions I can't even imagine. Add that to this crazy family legacy and, well, I've got to cut him some slack on this one."

"True. I have not walked a mile in Tripp's shoes." He looked at me questioningly.

I smiled. "Yes, it's the kind of prosthetic that allows him to wear two shoes. I think, if he had been wearing pants instead of shorts, I still wouldn't have known."

"You know, I'm inclined to not like the guy. Knowing he's a veteran does not change the fact he's a jerk."

I started to protest, but he continued.

"But he is protective of his sister, and I can respect that. He may have other redeeming qualities."

This time I just gave him a look.

"You and I are friends. I will probably see more of him once you two work things out. I will try harder to get along."

"And there's also the Kaitlyn thing."

"What Kaitlyn thing? What have you heard?" he asked.

I hid my smile. "Nothing. I thought the two of you were getting along pretty well."

"I told her my cell number last time, but she may have forgotten it." He ducked his head shyly.

"True. The in-and-out book experience can be a little disconcerting if you're not used to it. When I start texting Tripp again, I'll get her number for you."

Aunt Biddy stuck her head into the storeroom. "Gregorio, you go back up front so I can talk to Penny."

I smiled at him apologetically. "We'll talk later."

He repositioned the chair he'd been using so Aunt Biddy could sit.

"Thank you, dear." She patted him on the arm then shooed him out the door. "Now, what's this about you finally meeting your BBF yesterday?" She certainly got right to the point.

"BBF?"

"Book boyfriend. You're young. You should keep up better."

"Makes sense. I had no idea you were so cool, Aunt Biddy."

She sighed. "No one does. Pity. Come on, spill it. I'm not getting any younger here."

"I'm not sure how much Bobbie told you…"

"Nothing. Sent me to get it from the source."

"Bobbie and I decided to take a girls' trip to track down the descendant I discovered in my research. You knew I've been trying to trace the families of the three guys Elizabeth mentioned, right?"

She nodded, so I continued.

"Well, we pulled into town, and there was his name, splashed across the building."

She eyed me skeptically.

"It's true! I mean, it was his gun store, but his name was right on it. And 'Tripp' is distinctive. If his name had been 'Bob', I wouldn't have given it a second glance. Anyway, it looks like Tripp is the one."

"Of course, he's the one; otherwise, he wouldn't be in the books."

"No, I mean he's the descendant. He'll be the one to end the curse or satisfy the magic if that's truly the solution. The guy we were tracking down is Tripp's dad."

"How about that!" Biddy slapped her knee. "I could tell he was a good Irish boy."

"You couldn't know that. He just looks American. He doesn't look anymore Irish than me."

Biddy took in my fair skin and the freckles sprinkling my nose. "You sure don't look Czech like me, girly."

I smiled, then told her all about Bobbie's and my latest adventure.

"Uh-mmm," she chastised. "You shouldn't leave that boy hanging."

Hmm. Same beat, different drummer. "I think we both needed time to work things out alone."

"That's a dumb idea. In my day, we didn't have that luxury. Two dates and a couple kisses and it was a done deal. We had problems, we worked them out together. Start as you plan to continue."

I questioned Biddy's rendition of the past. She married in the 60s, after all, but I didn't call her on it. What she said had merit.

"We'll work it out," I said confidently.

"You left. You proved everything he expected to happen. He's going to put up walls to protect himself from more hurt. Men are proud creatures. They won't open themselves up to being hurt twice."

"We both need time," I said again, but with less confidence.

"Absence doesn't make the heart grow fonder, girly. That's a flat lie. Absence makes the brain fabricate all kinds of lies to tell the heart. You better make things right with that boy, and quick."

I hugged the older woman. "I will, Aunt Biddy, I promise."

****

I dreamed about my gram last night. It had been a long while since the last time when she told me to find her letters.

This time, she was walking around the bookshop. It looked like it does now, except all of her crazy lamps were back. She turned them on one by one. "You've got a decision to make," she said.

"What decision?" Though I thought I knew.

"You need to either be all-in or let it go."

"How can I let it go? This is a chance to end the magic, once and for all. If he's my soul mate, supposedly I can't achieve true happiness with anyone else. I don't really have the option to let it go."

"That's what really bothers you, isn't it? You don't want to make your own choices, but you resent the choices that have been made for you, despite their rightness."

I shrugged.

"You're stuck in this bookstore for a year, but it's not your passion. You've met someone who could be the love of your life but don't want to risk your whole heart because he wasn't your choice. Throw in a few obstacles like geography and sins of omission, and they make easy excuses to let him go."

"Our relationship is new. I don't know if it's strong enough to handle long-distance plus Tripp's insecurities."

"Your silence only feeds his insecurities; that's why you're stronger together. I release you from the bookstore. It was my connection to your grandfather. I only wanted you to have time to give the magic a chance. Sell it, turn it into one of those fancy cafés, whatever. I give you permission to pack up your e-reader and never look back."

"You can't do that. You're a figment of my imagination!" Gram finished turning on all the lamps in the shop and the place was lit up like Times Square. In the light, she sure didn't look like a figment.

"Figure out what you love. What makes you happy outside of any other relationships. Discover that, then when you add the relationship back in, you'll feel more complete rather than obligated. Don't count on a man to make you happy, but to share something you already have."

I hoped this rationalization actually originated from

my brain. First, because it meant I'd be able to access the info later, and second because I'd hate for Gram to have left the glories of heaven just to put her idiot granddaughter on the right path. Regardless, I went in for a hug I'd been sorely missing. "Thank you, Gram. I miss you."

She squeezed me tight. "I miss you too, Penny-pie. You'll figure it out. Find your joy."

I rolled over in my bed and cracked one eye open. The sky over top of the buildings across the street was turning a peachy-blush color. It was time to find my joy.

Chapter 24

It's My Pity Party

"Has Penny called yet?" Kaitlyn asked after she'd invited herself up to my apartment for lunch. I sprawled in my recliner, ignoring the beer I knew sat in the back of my fridge. There were only two, not near enough to drown my troubles. Besides, my counselor warned me off that route every time I saw her.

Instead, I chose oblivion via home improvement shows. That might have been a worse choice, watching happy couples building and renovating homes of their dreams. All that happiness made me feel worse than a hangover, but I still couldn't bring myself to shut it off.

What were Penny's goals and dreams? I should probably know by now. We couldn't build a life on chemistry and my lies. I knew she had a degree she didn't really know what to do with and a used bookstore, but I didn't feel like she had a real passion for that either.

Kaitlyn crossed her arms and leaned her hip against the sofa. "I shouldn't feel bad for you; you totally brought it on yourself. But I haven't seen you this pathetic since you moved back home."

"I haven't felt this hopeless since then. I finally got my life to a point where I felt purpose again, then she came and made me think I could have more. Now, what I used to be happy with, doesn't fill me up anymore."

"So quit wallowing and go get her!"

"She asked for time. After what I did, I can at least give her time to figure out if she wants to bother with me."

"Gah! You are such a knucklehead. She is, too, for that matter. But I can't help her with whatever her issues are. One thing I know, she doesn't care about your leg. She doesn't think you're half a man or whatever crazy scenario you're cooking up in your stupid head. She's giving you time to stop thinking so poorly of yourself and her." Kaitlyn paused, working something through her brain. "Though that sounds like a pretty weak reason for ghosting you. Bobbie can deal with her; you're my problem."

"I'm nobody's problem but my own. I don't need you." I scowled and flipped the channel to a cooking show, my other new vice.

She moved an empty pizza box and sat down on the couch, close to my chair. "Tripp, what do you want? Forget about your leg; forget about Penny for now. What do you want your life to look like ten years from now?"

I pursed my lips and glared at her. "I want a house that I built, or at least designed myself. I want a little land. I don't know for what, but I want to have options. I want a relationship like mom and dad's. I want a kid, eventually."

"How does a prosthetic keep you from doing any of those things?"

"Physically, it doesn't, but who wants all the baggage that goes with it? I lied to someone I'm falling in love with. Who does that?"

"People do lots of things to protect themselves. You've got to give Penny a chance to know you a

150

hundred percent, not just the parts that are easy to share."

"I guess the ball's in her court now. There's nothing I can do until she's ready to talk to me."

"Possibly. But there might be something we can do to help facilitate things."

"Like what?"

"Oh, I'm sorry, Trippy. By 'we', I meant me."

****

"I have them!" Kaitlyn let herself into my apartment.

"Have what?" I probably sounded grumpy, but that's what she gets for coming over uninvited. I still hadn't heard from Penny, so I spent most of my non-working hours wallowing in a pissy mood.

"Bobbie sent me the last pages of *Chase the Night*."

I sat up in my chair and turned off the muted television. "Why did she send them to you?"

"We chatted. Since it appears we care more for you and Penny's emotional health than you two do, we figured out what needed to happen at the end of the book for you two to have closure."

"Closure? Who said anything about closure? Penny said we need a little time to figure things out. Give me those."

She skipped back out of my reach. "Uh, uh! You can't read them; we'll get sucked in. You have to wait until tomorrow night. And by closure, I meant figure out how to move forward or whatever."

Kaitlyn was playing devil's advocate, but she still managed to rile me up. No one knew Penny better than Bobbie. "What do the pages say?"

"The vampire leaves her behind because she's slowing him down. The wolf and I chase after him, and

151

you are so glad to have her back, you discuss your relationship. Actually, that part is supposed to be kissing and professing your love, but you guys need to talk, so you can go off-script for as long as you need. It's kind of an anticlimactic ending since the reader never finds out if the vampire is caught. Bobbie and I thought the reconciliation of the main characters more important. We're hoping it's written in a way that will satisfy the magic." Kaitlyn shrugged like it wasn't a big deal that I may or may not be afforded an undetermined amount of time to convince the girl I probably love to overlook my lying and brokenness and give me another chance.

"What time tomorrow?"

"I told Bobbie I'd make sure you were home by eight-thirty."

It had been almost a week since our in-person meeting. Now I had less than twenty-four hours to figure out what to say. What could I say to convince Penny I was a good bet when I couldn't even convince myself?

Chapter 25

Discover Your Love In Books

Chase the Night

"Stacia, come with me. You will be my queen!" Though the vampire held Stacia's arm in an iron grip, he was careful not to bruise her skin.

"Can't you see, Lucien? I don't want to give up my mortality, and I don't love you. If you care for me as much as you say, you'll want me to be happy."

"With that hunter?" DeFrost spat.

"I don't know. But if you keep me against my will, he will never stop hunting you. And if you turn me, I will never forgive you. I will give up my life if you force me to give up my dreams and my ability to walk in the daylight. Not to mention, I'm a vegetarian. I'd have to give up my ideals if I chose life with you."

Shouts and barks from below filled Stacia with new urgency. "Lucien, you've been kind to me. I don't want to see you hurt." The vampire snorted at the absurdity. "Please, let me go and save yourself."

Lucien let go of her arm and brought her hand to his lips. He grazed one fang over her knuckle before pressing a kiss to the back. "We will meet again, possibly as enemies. Is that what you want?"

"It's the way it has to be." I doubled over in laughter. When I finally caught my breath I said, "Bobbie, that had

153

to be the corniest dialogue ever!"

"You promised not to criticize anymore. You know what I've had to work with." Her voice seemed to echo in the sky.

Peter looked at me with a goofy grin, mostly due to his fangs hanging out over his lips. "Well, I'm gonna make like a tree." He started backing away.

I heard panting behind me. Kaitlyn, followed closely by Gregorio in wolf form, crested the hill. "We're…coming." The panting was coming from her, not the canine.

"See ya at the beach!" Peter gave them a mock salute, turned, and sprinted off faster than humanly possible.

Kaitlyn groaned. "I am *not* running. You can if you want."

Wolf Gregorio whined, but stuck close to her leg as they started toward the trees.

"Good luck!" Kaitlyn waved and they disappeared into the trees.

I turned back to the path where they had emerged. Tripp stood there. Mentally, I compared this Tripp to the one I met in Granite Mount. I saw Lieutenant Culver Eberhart and Steve, star basketball player, and vampire hunter, Thorne. All of those characters were a little bit Tripp. He was protective, chivalrous, kind, smart, a little arrogant, and self-important. Well, maybe not the last one. The opposite, actually; he didn't see himself as important enough.

"Hey." He shoved his hands deep into the pockets of his leather duster.

"Hey. I'm sorry I didn't call. I didn't want to do this over the phone."

"I get it. No one likes to be dumped that way. I appreciate your consideration."

"What? I'm not dumping you. I just needed time to work some things out for myself."

"Right. And give me time to think about my own transgressions."

I kept telling myself he was being an ass to protect his tender heart, not because he was really an ass. "No. Maybe. I needed you to think about why you felt like you couldn't share the truth with me."

"It took me a long time after I got home to figure out what to do with my life. I had a lot of mental and physical baggage to overcome. No, scratch that, not overcome, learn to live with. My leg and my failure overseas will always be with me."

"Hold up. What failure?"

"My platoon was ripped apart by a roadside bomb. I led us right into it."

"So, identifying hidden bombs was solely your responsibility?"

"No, but—"

"And every veteran out there missing a limb because of an enemy attack is a failure as well?"

"No. Listen—"

"No. I know what kind of person you are, and I see how you could interpret your situation as a failure. But it wasn't and you're not. You only failed if you let your past keep you from enjoying your life. I'm pretty sure the military is fond of accountability. If no one told you what happened was your fault," I paused, and he shook his head. "Then you have to stop taking on the blame."

"My therapist may have said the same thing." His shoulders fell.

"Then let it go. Someone recently told me to find my joy, and everything else that matters will fall into place." I took several steps forward until I was within arm's reach of him.

"I'm not going to be able to drop everything all at once. And I can't promise I'll never pick it up again."

"I know," I said softly. I reached out and laid my hand on his upper arm. "And when it's more than you can carry alone, you have someone with you to help carry the load and unpack it."

Tripp finally pulled his hands from his pockets and rested them on my waist. "Find my joy?"

I smiled. "Find your joy."

"What about us?"

"Find your joy, and the rest will fall into place."

"I'm going to hold you to that."

"You can bet on it." His lips met mine and we sealed the deal.

Epilogue

Ten months later

I walked up the center aisle with measured steps.
The park turned out to be the perfect location for the
ceremony. The trees were green with new leaves and the
ground no longer squishy; though my heels still sank
with every step. When I reached the end, I took my place
opposite Gregorio.

He smiled at me, looking so handsome in his crisp
linen suit. I took a deep breath in an effort to hold back
tears. Ugh! Weddings and funerals, every time! Why do
I think I can get through either without tissues?

Gregorio pulled a fresh white hanky out of an inside
pocket and handed it to Peter who mopped his brow,
neck, and started to go for his armpits until Gregorio
gently tugged his sleeve and shook his head once. Peter
handed the used fabric back to its owner, to which
Gregorio shook his head again. Peter gave his face one
more swipe before stuffing the hanky into his pants
pocket.

The music changed and everyone rose and turned.
Bobbie and her father started down the aisle. She wore
an ivory lace dress that had been her grandmother's. A
fantastic seamstress altered the dated original into a slim-
fitting, sleeveless design. I was a little envious. All of her
dark brown hair was piled artfully on top of her head and

though she preferred her glasses, she wore contacts in deference to wedding photos.

When they reached us, she gave her father a kiss and handed me her bouquet of lilies and roses. Then she turned and took Peter's hands. The rest of the ceremony was a familiar blur. She didn't burden Peter by making him write his own vows, so everything went by the book. Gregorio handed over the rings and the couple was pronounced Mr. and Mrs. Celansky.

After the ceremony the photographer took pictures by the pond, and the flowerbeds, and the pretty tree, and the rock wall. Then he took a variety of artful shots of Bobbie and me and Peter and Gregorio. By the time we were finished I was ready for reception food. The Celanskys sent the guests ahead to start without them. No one liked warm cold cuts and cold side dishes.

Only two vehicles waited, the limo to transport the wedding party and Tripp's pick up.

"Congratulations, guys; beautiful ceremony." Tripp shook Peter's hand and kissed Bobbie lightly on the cheek.

"Where's Kaitlyn?" I asked. She rode with us to the ceremony. She lived in my old apartment and managed the bookshop. She'd done amazing things with the space and had instituted several *real* book clubs. She rearranged the shelves and also offered BYOB painting and craft classes on weekend evenings.

"She went on with Aunt Biddy to make sure everyone got started and found seats."

"We'd better get over there." Bobbie started toward the limo. "Pictures took way longer than I thought they would."

"I'll follow with Penny, if that's okay with you."

Tripp took my hand.

"No problem, bro." Peter slapped him on the back as he walked by.

"See you there," Gregorio added. I was glad they had finally settled into a grudging friendship. Kaitlyn told them they didn't have a choice and I suspected one day they might end up brothers-in-law.

"What's up?" I asked as the limo pulled away.

"I got you a present. Come on." He pulled me over to the last row of folding chairs so I could get off my feet. Sadly, my shoes were already ruined by the mud by the pond, but I'd be unlikely to wear the buttery yellow kitten heels again. My bridesmaid dress was the only thing I owned that matched them. Once I was seated, Tripp pulled a slim, wrapped rectangle out of his inside pocket.

I unwrapped it to find an old, gently used volume of poetry with a blue sticky note marking a spot about halfway through. I never read poetry, and to my knowledge, neither did Tripp. "What's this?"

"Read the poem where it's marked."

I eyed him skeptically but did as instructed.

Garden of Love
I walk through the garden with my lady love.
The sun sparkles off each dew drop
Ivy creeps languidly around trees and rock
Silently battling with mossy hair.
Lilac and honeysuckle scent the air
We meander down paths guided only by whim
Willow branches open to invite us in.

As I read, the park around us transformed into the picturesque garden described on the page. I'd no idea the legacy would work with poetry, let alone terrible poetry.

This is the destination I seek
I guide her to sit and drop to one knee.

Finally, my chair turned into a stone bench under a massive weeping willow and Tripp was in front of me, like the poem said, down on one knee. "Oh, Tripp," I whispered on a breath.

"You have no idea how much bad poetry Kaitlyn and I had to sift through to find this gem. This is why I haven't had you out to my trailer in the past few months. There are books stacked everywhere." Tripp was in the process of building a house and lived in an RV on site. "I almost resorted to writing my own but couldn't come up with any fancy words or make them rhyme. I also wondered if publication might be a factor in getting the magic to work."

"This is perfect. Gram would have been so impressed with you." I ran my fingers through his hair and cupped his cheek. I was touched he went through the effort to make this so special for me. Seeing him balanced on one knee, I wondered if this wasn't also for himself.

Would we still be able to book walk after we were married like Gram and Gramp did, just for fun? Or would the magic be over? For Tripp's sake, I hoped we'd still be able to do this, but I was jumping the gun. My man was still on one knee waiting patiently for my full attention. "This is perfect," I repeated.

"Penelope Darling, will you give up your freedom and leg shackle yourself to me until the end of our days?"

"Tripp Wendell Francis Kinney." He cringed at my use of his full name. "I would be thrilled to become your wife and be with you forever with the bonus of freeing the women of my line from the gypsy magic Elizabeth bought so long ago. Being shackled to you is going to be a lot more fun than being shackled to a legacy. I love you."

"I love you too, Penn, so much." He rose and dug a gorgeous one-carat low profile solitaire set in a smooth black tungsten band out of his pocket. "Cool, I hoped this would work. I was afraid I'd have to present you with the ring in the poem, but this is the one I picked out. I figured the best way to match your grandmother's ring was to not try to match it at all. I hope this is okay."

"It's more than okay." He slipped it on to my finger. "I love it, and I love that you got a style I'll be less likely to damage or muck up at work." I had taken over his old apartment above his parent's garage and worked part time at the Gypsy Falls Riding Stables. The other part of the time I was back in school working toward a degree in physical therapy with a focus on hippotherapy. Of course, I kissed him then.

"Um, Penn, we've never done a poem before, so I don't exactly know how we get out of it."

"How much longer does it go after the knee part?"

"It went on for a couple pages of the guy trying to convince his lady love what a great catch he was. Thanks for not making me do that."

"Hmm. Then I think we should enjoy this beautiful, but poorly written setting for as long as it lasts. I'm starving, but not in any hurry to sit through endless toasts only to finish with following Aunt Biddy through a conga line."

He laughed. "I'm game, as long as I'm with you." He took my hand and led me into the garden.

"Always," I replied. "'Til the very last page."

Check out this preview of Book 4 in the In for a Penny Series: *Penny Ante*

Chapter 1

Lonesome Dove

I clenched my fist, willing myself not to knock, as I stood outside Mabel's apartment. How many more times would I put myself through it? Despite living in neighboring towns and our families being close, I'd managed to avoid spending quality time with the girl who'd locked me in the friend zone.

But I always came if she truly needed me, like now, when Axel Doucheman's broken her heart. I've picked up the pieces of her heart enough times, you'd think I would own a bigger part of it. I sighed. I'd already driven across town, and it wasn't like I had any big plans for spring break anyway. I let my fist fall against the door.

I heard movement from the other side, encouraged that it wasn't wild sobbing. The chains rattled and the deadbolt turned before the door swung open revealing the familiar red eyes and puffy cheeks of my best friend.

"Sam!" Mabel flung herself into my arms.

I tensed, then let myself return the embrace. "I brought rocky road." I lifted the plastic sack in my hand.

Mabel hiccuped as a sob escaped. "You're always there for meee…" Her words trailed off as she buried her face in my chest.

A door opened down the hall.

"Come on, weepy," I said as I penguin-walked her backwards through the door. "Go sit on the couch while I put this in your freezer."

She sat and pulled a blanket over her head. The coffee table and floor were littered with crumpled tissues. I shook my head. I would never understand how such a smart, vibrant, confident girl—woman could let herself get so torn up over guys that weren't good enough for her.

I'd given the topic more thought than was probably healthy. She had a great family. My Uncle Tripp was awesome and always there for his kids, so no daddy-abandonment issues there. The only reasonable explanation I could come up with was Mabel's hopeless romanticism. She was in love with being in love. When the losers showed their true colors or realized they couldn't live up to her expectations, they checked out.

I found bowls in the cabinet and scooped out rocky road for her and vanilla I'd gotten for myself and prepared myself for a long night. I carried the bowls to the living room. Not much had changed in her apartment since her move-in party the previous summer. A footlocker, a newer version of the one in the tree house, still sat under the window where I'd placed it. Pictures hung on the wall: some artsy pieces I knew Bertie had painted and family photos. A rush of emotion squeezed my heart when I saw a photo of the two of us from my high school graduation included in the display.

"What happened with Doucheman?" I asked as I settled beside her.

She sniffed. "Dorfman."

"Po-tay-toes, po-tah-toes. Has he gone the way of the dodo?"

"You're so weird." She scooted closer and leaned against me. "No glasses today?"

"Not much anymore." Though I had them with me in case I ended up crashing on the sofa. "Quit changing the subject."

"We planned for me to go with him to Boise over spring break. But yesterday he said he felt like we were in different places and thought we should take a break."

I gritted my teeth. "That's not so bad. You don't want to rush in to meeting his parents." I'd met Doucheman once when she brought him home for Thanksgiving several months ago. I wasn't a fan.

"I've been told by three other guys that we should take a break, and every time what they mean is a breakup." She commenced on a renewed crying jag.

I leaned back so I could put an arm around her shoulders. I was made of sterner stuff than most men my age in that female tears didn't bother me. Well, Mabel's break-up tears didn't bother me, at least. I'd learned a long time ago they represented the cleansing of yet another loser from her life. It used to give me hope she'd finally realize best friends made the best partners. After living this exact scenario six or seven times, I learned Mabel would never see me that way without a grand gesture on my part. I wouldn't risk our friendship like that.

"Your sofa is a lot more comfortable for this than your tree house," I teased.

She grabbed the tissue box from the table and blew her nose. "We had some good times up there, though."

"Yeah, we did, before you became a teenage

watering pot."

She smacked my chest, a good sign the worst was coming to an end. "You had your share of tears up there."

"Never!" I laughed. If she only knew how I'd pined for her.

"Remember when we used to play book?"

"Sure. It was all we ever did. Turned me into an avid reader, though."

"I think Aunt Bobbie did that." Mabel laughed. "I finally got around to looking through that box."

"What box?"

"Remember when I told you my mom said all the stories were real? There's a gypsy curse and a family legacy. It's how my parents met."

"You didn't tell me that. You said it was boring books and old lady letters and you thought your mom had a psychotic break." I reluctantly lifted her off me so I could see her face.

"I finally got around to reading everything. It's a pretty elaborate hoax if it's not real. Your mom told you stories, too. There was a whole notebook full of magic rules that she wrote."

"Really?" My mom was not what you'd consider fanciful.

"Yeah. All the books were the ones my ancestresses had 'read' into. That's what our moms called it, 'reading-in' to the stories. They would read and then they'd literally be in the story. There was a family tree all the way back to the 1700s for both my mom and my dad and letters, really old ones, that all backed up what mom said."

Mabel spoke the truth, or at least she believed what she told me. Gypsy magic wasn't real. "Where is all this stuff?" I needed hard evidence.

"Mom still has it."

I grabbed a paperback from underneath a pile of tissues. "You're saying, if you open this and start reading, we'll both magically be in the story? Where's this guy's shirt anyway?"

"Give me that!" She made a grab for it, but I held it out of reach.

"*Love's Gamble*. Will Rose take a gamble on love? Ooh." I made immature kissing noises. "Answer the question, Mabes."

She crossed her arms. "No. I'd end up in the story with my true love."

Ouch. "Of course."

"It doesn't work anymore, anyway. Mom found my dad and he is the descendant of my great, great, great, great grandmother Elizabeth's destined true love."

My arm slackened. "Your parents are related?"

Mabel made another swipe at the book, so I raised it again. "No, pay attention. Elizabeth didn't marry her destined true love. She married a gypsy man." She expelled a breath. "It's a long story. Give me my book back and I'll explain."

"Maybe you have so many man troubles because you read this garbage. It gives you unrealistic expectations."

She rolled her eyes. "Quit being a brat."

"What's it even about? He's wearing a cowboy hat. I think cowboys usually wear shirts, especially back in the days when women wore dresses like that. Hers appears to be missing a few buttons, though."

"Sam..." I ignored her warning tone. "I don't know what it's about; I'm not very far."

"Well, let's see. I opened it with one hand to the page with the dog-eared corner. "Chapter two. That's pretty far."

"Fine. The heroine is trying to save her ranch after her parents died. There's a slimy dude trying to woo it away from her."

"Ah ha! Enter the hero, sans shirt," I teased. "Ah hem. Clifton McGrath dragged himself across the barren landscape…"

Love's Gamble

…he hoped his faithful steed, Bolt, would find his way back to Cliff eventually. He was a smart horse, but even the best mount will spook at the sight of a rattler in its path.

Left with nothing but his shirt on his back and his pistol, he was soon relieved of those as well by a band of thieves. Took his boots, too. Cliff was in a right sorry way. When a dilapidated ranch house appeared in the distance, his poor luck led him to believe it was nothing but a mirage. Two days without water would do that to a man.

The creak of the windmill and dresses flapping on the clothesline made for a mighty detailed mirage. The barking mutt that ran out to scare him off finally convinced him of its reality.

He smoothed back his dark brown hair and wiped a hand down his face, embarrassed to encounter a week's growth of stubble. There would be no improving his appearance. He'd just have to depend on the rancher's Christian character and generous disposition.

The dog ceased barking and followed close at Cliff's heels as he climbed the steps to the porch. He clenched his fist, regretting the circumstances leading him to this point, and let it rap against the roughhewn door.

He glanced at his surroundings while he waited. He would offer to work in exchange for food, water, a bath, and a shirt. It looked like an older couple hadn't been able to keep up with the day to day needs of a working ranch, or perhaps the hands were slacking. He'd be glad to help for a few days while he recovered and reclaimed his bearings.

The door opened. Cliff spun back to greet not a bent old man, but a young woman with wild auburn hair and fire in her eyes to match.

"Damn it, Sam. What have you done?"

A word about the author...

Shelley is a twenty-five-year resident of Oklahoma with roots in Maine. She and her husband have four awesome kids, but are thrilled three have successfully reached adulthood and moved out. She spends her time working, writing, reading, baking, sewing, and exercising just enough to counteract her other activities.

In for a Penny is the third book in her series of the same name. She would be ever so grateful if you would consider leaving a review when you finish this partially paranormal romance.

www.shelleywhitewrites.com
facebook.com/shelleywhiteauthor

Thank you for purchasing
this publication of The Wild Rose Press, Inc.

For questions or more information
contact us at
info@thewildrosepress.com.

The Wild Rose Press, Inc.
www.thewildrosepress.com